HARLEQUIN®
Presents~

Take time out from your busy schedule this month to kick back and relax with a brand-new Harlequin Presents novel. We hope you enjoy this month's selection.

If you love royal heroes, you're in for a treat this month! In Penny Jordan's latest book, *The Italian Duke's Wife,* an Italian aristocrat chooses a young English woman as his convenient wife. When he unleashes within her a desire she never knew she possessed, he is soon regretting his no-consummation rule.... Emma Darcy's sheikh in *Traded to the Sheikh* is an equally powerful and sexy alpha male. This story has a wonderfully exotic desert setting, too!

We have some gorgeous European men this month. *Shackled by Diamonds* by Julia James is part of our popular miniseries GREEK TYCOONS. Read about a Greek tycoon and the revenge he plans to exact on an innocent, beautiful model when he wrongly suspects her of stealing his priceless diamonds. In Sarah Morgan's *Public Wife, Private Mistress,* can a passionate Italian's marriage be rekindled when he is unexpectedly reunited with his estranged wife?

In *The Antonides Marriage Deal* by Anne McAllister, a Greek magnate meets a stunning new business partner, and he begins to wonder if he can turn their business arrangement into a permanent contract—such as marriage! Kay Thorpe's *Bought by a Billionaire* tells of a Portuguese billionaire and his ex-lover. He wants her back as his mistress. Previously she rejected his proposal because of his arrogance and his powerful sexuality. But this time he wants marriage....

Happy reading! Look out for a brand-new selection next month.

Surrender To The Sheikh

Emma Darcy

TRADED TO THE SHEIKH

Surrender To
The Sheikh

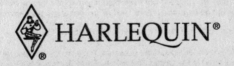

HARLEQUIN®

TORONTO • NEW YORK • LONDON
AMSTERDAM • PARIS • SYDNEY • HAMBURG
STOCKHOLM • ATHENS • TOKYO • MILAN • MADRID
PRAGUE • WARSAW • BUDAPEST • AUCKLAND

ISBN 0-373-12530-5

TRADED TO THE SHEIKH

First North American Publication 2006.

Copyright © 2005 by Emma Darcy.

This edition published by arrangement with Harlequin Books S.A.

www.eHarlequin.com

Printed in U.S.A.

All about the author...
Emma Darcy

EMMA DARCY was born in Australia, and currently lives on a beautiful country property in New South Wales. Her ambition to be an actress was partly satisfied by playing in amateur theater productions, but ultimately fulfilled in becoming a writer, where she has the exciting pleasure of playing all the roles!

Initially a teacher of French and English, she changed her career to computer programming before marriage and motherhood settled her into a community life. Her creative urges were channeled into oil painting, pottery, designing and overseeing the construction and decorating of two homes, all in the midst of keeping up with three lively sons and the very busy social life of her businessman husband.

A voracious reader, the step to writing her own books seemed natural and the challenge of creating wonderful stories was soon highly addictive. With her strong interest in people and relationships, Emma found the world of romance fiction a happy one. Currently, she has broadened her horizons and begun to write mainstream women's fiction.

Her conviction that we must make all we can out of the life we are given keeps her striving to know more, be more and give more—this is reflected in all her books.

CHAPTER ONE

SHEIKH ZAGEO bin Sultan Al Farrahn was not amused.
Not only had there been criminal trespassing in the
walled grounds of this family property—his mother's
pleasure palace on the legendary spice island of
Zanzibar—but also criminal use of the private harbour
by a drug-running French yachtsman who was actually
offering him a woman to warm his bed in exchange for
letting him go.

Did the sleazy low-life think he was speaking to the
kind of man who'd indulge in indiscriminate sex?

'She's very special,' the drug-dealer pleaded with all
the oiliness of a practised pimp. 'A genuine strawberry-
blonde. Hair like rippling silk, falling to the pit of her back.
Beautiful, bright, blue eyes. Lush breasts…' His hands
shaped an hourglass figure. 'Fantastic legs, long and…'

'A virgin, as well?' Zageo cut in mockingly, despis-
ing the man for thinking he could trade his whore for
his own freedom, for thinking the trade could even be
an acceptable possibility.

'Completely untouched,' Jacques Arnault instantly replied, a consummate liar, not so much as a flicker of an eyelash nor the twitch of a facial muscle to betray any unease with the question, despite the impossibility of there being anything virginal about a woman who had to be his partner in crime.

'And where is this precious pearl?' Zageo drawled, barely holding back his contempt for a man who was prepared to sell flesh to save his own skin.

'On my yacht. If you get your security people—' he glanced nervously at the guards who'd caught him '—to take me out to it, they can fetch her back to you.'

While he silently sailed away in one hell of a hurry!

Zageo gave him a blast of scepticism. 'On your yacht? You've managed to sail from the Red Sea, down half the east coast of Africa to this island, without being tempted to touch this fabulous jewel of femininity?'

The Frenchman shrugged. 'Stupid to spoil top merchandise.'

'And where did you get this *top merchandise*?'

'Picked her up from one of the resorts where she was working with a dive team. She agreed to help crew the yacht for free passage to Zanzibar.' His mouth curved into a cynical smile. 'A drifting traveller who could go missing indefinitely.'

'A fool to trust you with her life.'

'Women are fools. Particularly those with an innocent turn of mind.'

Zageo arched a challenging eyebrow. 'You take me for a fool, as well?'

'I'm being completely straight with you,' came the swift and strongly assertive assurance. 'You can have her. No problems.' His gaze flicked around the lavishly rich and exotic Versace furnishings in the huge central atrium which had always served as the most public reception area. 'With all you have to offer, I doubt you'd even have to force her. Unless you enjoy force, of course,' he quickly added on second thoughts.

Anger burned. 'You are breaking another law, monsieur. The slave trade was abolished in Zanzibar over a century ago.'

'But a man of your standing and influence…who's to question what you do with a woman no one knows? Even if she runs away from you…'

'Enough!' Zageo gestured to his security guards. 'Put him in a holding room. Have his yacht searched for a woman. If there is one onboard, bring her to me.'

Arnault looked alarmed as two of the guards flanked him to escort him elsewhere. He spoke quickly in anxious protest. 'You'll see. She's everything I said she is. Once you're satisfied…'

'Oh, I will be satisfied, monsieur, one way or another,' Zageo silkily assured him, waving his men to proceed with the execution of his orders.

Zageo doubted the woman existed, certainly not with all the attributes ascribed to her by Jacques Arnault. He suspected the Frenchman had been dangling what he thought would be a tempting sexual fantasy in the hope of getting back to his yacht and somehow ditching the men escorting him. Even though the security guards carried guns, a surprise attack might have won him time to escape.

However, if there was a female accomplice, she had to be brought in and handed over to the appropriate authorities. While she might not have been actively involved in drug-dealing, there was no way she couldn't know about it and would surely be able to supply useful information.

He relaxed back on the thronelike sofa, reached over the elaborately rolled armrest to pick up the mango cocktail he'd previously set down on the entwined monkeys table, and sipped the refreshing drink slowly as the anger stirred by the Frenchman's attempt to use sexual currency turned onto Veronique, who had declined the invitation to accompany him on this trip.

'Your mind will be on business, *cheri*,' she had prettily complained. 'It will not be fun.'

Was the amount of *fun* to be had the measure of their relationship? His three-month tour of checking the hotel chain he'd established throughout Africa could not be called a hardship on anyone's agenda—luxurious resorts in exotic locations. How much *fun* did she need to feel happy and satisfied?

He understood that for the much-in-demand French-Morrocan model, pleasure was inextricably linked with exciting leisure and being taken shopping. He understood that what he provided in this context was the trade-off for having her as his mistress. He had not understood that Veronique was only prepared to give him her company on her own totally self-indulgent terms.

Intolerable!

He had indulged her far too much. It wasn't enough recompense that the sex was good. It wasn't enough that Veronique was invariably a splendid ornament on his arm, superbly dressed to complement her dark-skinned exotic beauty. He found it deeply insulting that she had so little respect for *his* wishes.

His father was right. It was time he ended this too long fascination with women of different cultures and found one of his own kind to marry. He was thirty-five years old and should be thinking of settling down, having a family. He would cut his connection with Veronique and start considering more suitable candidates for a lifelong commitment—well-educated women from other powerful families in Dubai, women whose background ensured they would share his life, not just his bed and his spending power.

None of them would have strawberry-blond hair, blue eyes and fair skin, but such factors were hardly prime requirements for marriage. They weren't even factors to inspire a lustful dalliance. Right now the idea of trading in sex was particularly abhorrent, and Zageo found himself actually relishing the opportunity to hammer this home to Jacques Arnault's female yachting companion.

He hoped she did exist.

He hoped his men would find her on board the illicit yacht in the private harbour that served this private palace.

He hoped she actually measured up to the Frenchman's selling spiel.

It would give him considerable satisfaction to demonstrate that regardless of how attractive her physical assets were, they were worth nothing to him.

Absolutely nothing!

CHAPTER TWO

'I WILL get out of this! I will!' Emily Ross kept reciting as she struggled through the mangrove swamp.

These mutterings of fierce determination were interspersed with bursts of self-castigation. 'What a fool I've been! A gullible idiot to be taken in by Jacques. I should have just paid the money to fly here. No hassle about arriving in time. All safe and sound…'

Talking blocked out the fear of having made another wrong step, of putting her life in hopeless hazard this time. Yet reason insisted that the Frenchman could not have been trusted to keep his word about anything. The only sure way of staying in Zanzibar and getting to Stone Town to meet Hannah was to jump ship while Jacques was still off in his dinghy doing his drug-running.

So, okay…she'd done the swim from the yacht to shore, dragging all her essentials in a waterproof bag behind her. No shark or fish had attacked. Her feet had not been cut to ribbons by shells or coral or sharp rocks. Now she just had to find her way out of the mangrove swamp that seemed to cover the peninsula she'd swum to.

'It's not going to beat me. I *will* get out of it.'

And she did, finally emerging from the mud and tangled tree roots onto a wide mound of firmer ground which turned out to be an embankment above a small creek. More water! But beyond it was definitely proof of civilisation—what looked like the well kept grounds of some big property. No more swamp. The worst was over.

Emily's legs shook from sheer exhaustion. Now, with the fear of being swallowed up by the swamp receding and much easier travelling in sight, she felt like collapsing on the bank and weeping with relief at having made it this far. Nevertheless, the need to cling to some self-control persisted. She might be out of the woods but this was still far from the end of her journey.

She sat herself down on the bank and did some deep breathing, hoping to lessen the load of stress—the huge mental, emotional and physical stress attached to her decision not to cling to the relative safety of Jacques Arnault's yacht, not to remain captive to any further devious plan he might make.

Free…

The thought gathered its own momentum, finding a burst of positive achievement.

Free of him. Free of the swamp. Free to go where I want in my own time.

It helped calm her enough to get on with assessing her current position. A high stone wall ran back into distant darkness on the other side of the creek. It gave rise to the hope it might lead to a public road.

'If nothing else, it should give me cover until I'm right away from Jacques and his dirty business,' she muttered, trying to whip up the energy to move again.

Through sheer force of will, Emily drove her mind into forward planning as she heaved herself onto her feet and trudged along the bank of the creek until the stone wall was directly opposite her. Once across this last body of water, she could clean herself up and dress respectably in the skirt and T-shirt she'd placed at the top of the waterproof bag. Wearing a bikini at this time of night was hardly appropriate for meeting local people and sooner or later she had to confront someone in order to ask directions to Stone Town.

Waist-deep in water and hating every second of wading through it, Emily was concentrating on her footing when a commanding voice rang out.

'*Arretez!*'

The French verb to stop certainly stopped her!

She almost tripped in sheer shock.

Her heart jerked into a fearful hammering as her gaze whipped up to fix on two men pointing highly menacing rifles at her. They wore white shirts and trousers with black gun-belts, giving them more the appearance of official policemen than drug-running gangsters, but Emily wasn't sure if this was a good thing or a bad thing. If they'd caught Jacques and were connecting her to his criminal activities—which the use of French language suggested—she might end up in prison.

One of the men clapped a small mobile telephone to his ear and spoke at speed in what sounded like Arabic. The other motioned her to continue moving to their side of the creek bank. Having a rifle waved at her did not incline Emily towards disobedience. She could only hope these people were representatives of the law on this island and that the law would be reasonable in listening to her.

A giant fig tree on her left had obviously provided an effective hiding place for them to watch for her emergence from the mangroves. She wondered if other patrols were out looking for her. Certainly her appearance was being reported to someone. As she scrambled up their side of the creek bank, one of the men came forward and snatched the waterproof bag out of her grasp.

'Now hold on a moment! I've got my life in there!' Emily cried in panicky protest.

Having her passport, money and clothes taken from her was a very scary situation. Thinking the men might believe the bag contained contraband, she tried persuading them to check its contents.

'Look for yourself.' Her hands flew out in a gesture of open-palmed innocence. 'It's just personal stuff.'

No response. The men completely ignored her frantic attempt to communicate with them both in English and in her very limited tourist French. She was grabbed at the elbows and briskly marched across quite an expanse of mown grass to a path which eventually led to a massive three-storey white building.

At least it didn't look like a prison, Emily thought,

desperately trying to ·calm her wildly leaping apprehension. The many columned verandahs on each level, with their elaborate wrought-iron lace balustrades, gave the impression of British colonial architecture serving some important government purpose.

Maybe a courthouse?

But why on earth would Jacques do his drug-running right under the nose of legal officialdom?

Could it be terribly corrupt officialdom?

This thought frayed her strung-out nerves even further. She was a lone foreign woman, scantily dressed, and her only tool of protection was her passport which she no longer had in her possession. It took all her will-power not to give way to absolute panic when she was escorted up the steps to the front verandah and was faced with horribly intimidating entrance doors.

These were about four metres high, ominously black, intricately carved around the edges, and featuring rows of big pointed brass studs. They were definitely the kind of doors that would deter anyone from gate-crashing a party. As they were slowly swung open Emily instinctively decided that a bowed head and downcast eyes might get her into less trouble in this place.

The first sight she had of the huge foyer was of a gorgeous *Tree of Life* Persian rug dominating a dark wooden floor. As she was forced forward onto this carpet her side vision picked up the kind of splendid urns one might see in an art museum, which suggested this could be a *safe* environment.

A burst of hope prodded her into lifting her gaze to

check out where she was being taken. Her mind absolutely boggled at the scene rolling out in vivid Technicolor right in front of her. She was being led straight towards a huge central atrium, richly and exotically furnished in the style of a palatial reception area.

A walkway to the rest of the rooms on the ground floor surrounded the two-steps-down sunken floor of this incredible area, which was also overlooked by the balconies which ran around the second and third floors. Above it was a domed roof and from the circumference of the dome hung fantastic chandeliers of multicoloured glass that cascaded down in wonderful shapes and sizes.

As amazing as all this was, Emily's gaze almost instantly zeroed in on the man who was certainly the focal centrepiece of this totally decadent and fabulous luxury. He rose with majestic dignity from a thronelike sofa which was upholstered in red and gold. His clothes—a long white undertunic and a sleeveless overrobe in royal purple edged in gold braid—seemed to embrace Arabian culture but he didn't look like an Arab, more aristocratic Spanish. What wasn't in any doubt was that Emily was faced with the most stunningly beautiful man she had ever seen in her life.

Beautiful…

Strange word to apply to a man yet handsome somehow wasn't enough. The cast of his features was perfectly boned and balanced as though he was the creation of a mastor sculptor. A thick mane of straight black hair was swept back from his forehead, falling in shaggy layers to below his ears but not to shoulder-length. It was a bold and dramatic frame for a face that comprised brows which kicked up at a wicked angle, lending an emphatic effect to riveting dark eyes; a classically straight nose ending in a flare of nostrils that suggested a passionate temperament; a mouth whose upper lip was rather thin and sharply delineated while the lower lip was full and sensual.

The man fascinated, mesmerised, and although she thought of him as beautiful, there was an innate arrogant *maleness* to him that kicked a stream of primal fear through her highly agitated bloodstream. He was fabulous but also very foreign, and he was unmistakably assessing her female assets as he strolled forward, apparently for a closer examination.

Because he was at a lower floor level, Emily had the weird sense of catapulting back in time to the days when Zanzibar was the largest slave trading centre of the world, with herself being held captive on a platform for the buyers' appraisal.

He lifted a hand to seemingly flick a hair back from his forehead as he spoke in Arabic to one of the guards holding her. The scarf she'd tied around her head was suddenly snatched away, the rough movement dislodging the pins which had kept her hair in a twisted coil around her crown. The sheer weight of the untethered mass brought it tumbling down, spilling over her shoulders and down her back.

'Hey!' Emily cried in frightened protest, her imagination rioting towards being stripped of her bikini, as well. She was suddenly feeling extremely vulnerable, terrified of what his next command might be.

A burst of fluent French came from the Spaniard/Arab. It was accompanied by a cynical flash of his eyes and finished with a sardonic curl of his mouth. While Emily had picked up a smattering of quite a few languages on her travels, she was not up to comprehending this rush of foreign words and she didn't care for the expression that went with them, either.

'Look, I'm not French. Okay?' she pleaded. 'Any chance you speak English?'

'So—' one black eyebrow lifted in sceptical challenge '—you are English?'

'Well, no actually. I'm Australian. My name is Emily Ross.' She nodded to the waterproof bag still being held by one of her guards. 'My passport will prove…'

'Nothing of pertinent interest, madamoiselle,' he cut in drily.

Emily took a deep breath, pulling her wits together enough to address the *real* situation here. 'Then may I ask what *is* of pertinent interest to you, monsieur?'

He made an oddly graceful gesture suggesting a rather careless bit of interest he was just as happy to dismiss. 'Jacques Arnault gave a description of you which I find surprisingly accurate.' He spoke in a slow drawl, laced with irony, his eyes definitely mocking as he added, 'This has piqued my curiosity enough to inquire if he spoke more truth than I anticipated.'

'What did he claim?' Emily asked, her teeth clenching as she anticipated hearing a string of lies.

'That you are a virgin.'

A virgin!

Emily shut her eyes as her mind exploded with the shocking implications behind *her promised virginity*.

It could mean only one thing.

Jacques Arnault…who couldn't lie straight in bed at night even if he tried, the consummate con artist who'd tricked her into crewing on his yacht, the sneaky drug-runner who had no conscience about anything, whose mind was completely bent on doing whatever served his best interests…had obviously come up with a deal to save his own skin.

She was to be traded off as a sex slave!

'No!' she almost spat in fierce indignation, her eyes flying open to glare at the prospective buyer. 'Absolutely not!'

'I did not believe it,' he said with a dismissive shrug, the tone of his voice a very cold contrast to her heat. 'Since the evidence points to your being a professional belly-dancer, I'm sure you've had many patrons.'

'A professional belly-dancer?' Emily's voice climbed incredulously at this further off-the-wall claim.

He gave her an impatient look. 'Your costumes were found onboard Arnault's yacht, along with the other luggage you abandoned in fleeing from being associated with the Frenchman's criminal activities. Avoiding capture.'

Capture!

So Jacques had definitely been nabbed doing his drug-dealing, and his yacht subsequently searched, leading this man to think she'd twigged that the game was up and had taken to the water to escape being caught up in the mess.

'I was not fleeing from capture tonight, monsieur. I was fleeing from being a captive on that boat since it set sail from the Red Sea.'

'Jacques Arnault was holding you against your will?'

'Yes. And any belly-dancing costumes your search turned up do not belong to me, I assure you,' she stated heatedly, resenting the implied tag of being a professional whore, as well.

The heat in her voice slid right down her entire body as he observed in mocking detail every curve of her femininity; the voluptuous fullness of her breasts, the smallness of her waist, the broad sweep of her hips, the smooth flow and shape of her thighs, calves, ankles…

'Your physique suggests otherwise, Miss Ross,' he commented very dryly.

Emily burned. Her arms, released by the guards who were still flanking her, flew up to fold themselves protectively across her chest. Her chin lifted in belligerent pride as she stated, 'I'm a professional diving instructor. I have a certificate to prove it amongst my papers in the bag your men took from me.'

Her inquisitor smiled, showing a flash of very white teeth, but something about that smile told Emily he was relishing the prospect of tearing her into tasty morsels and chewing on them. 'It's my experience that people can be many things,' he remarked with taunting ease.

'Yes. Well, you're not wrong about that,' she

snapped. 'Jacques Arnault is a prime example. And I think it's time you told me who you are and what right you have to detain me like this.'

Emily was steaming with the need to challenge him, having been put so much on the spot herself. The idea of bowed head and downcast eyes was long gone. She kept a very direct gaze on his, refusing to back down from her demands.

'You were caught trespassing on property that belongs to my family and you are closely linked to a man who was engaged in criminal activity on this same property,' he clipped out as though her complaint was completely untenable—a total waste of time and breath.

'You have no evidence that *I* was engaged in criminal activity,' Emily swiftly defended.

He rolled his eyes derisively.

'I swear to you I wasn't,' she insisted. 'In fact, the costumes you found probably belong to the woman who posed as Jacques Arnault's wife when I was tricked into becoming the only crew member on his yacht.'

'Tricked, Miss Ross?'

'I needed to get to Zanzibar. Jacques said he was sailing for Madagascar and would drop me off here if I helped…'

'With his drug-running?'

'No. With sailing the yacht,' she cried in exasperation. 'I didn't know about the drug angle until after I woke up onboard and at sea, having been drugged myself.'

'So…' He paused, his expression one of weighing up her account of the situation. He lifted a hand to stroke his chin as though in thoughtful consideration. But there was something simmering in his eyes that sent a warning tingle through Emily's taut nerves as he concluded, '…you claim to be an innocent victim.'

'I *am* an innocent victim,' Emily pounced, swiftly asserting, 'The deal was for me to be company for his wife as well as being another crew-member for the duration of the trip.'

One wickedly derisive eyebrow arched. 'Where is the wife?'

Emily heaved a fretful sigh. Probably her story did sound unbelievable but it was the truth. She had nothing else to offer. 'I don't know. She was gone when I woke up the morning after I'd gone onboard.'

'Gone,' he repeated, as though underlining how convenient that was. 'Without taking her belly-dancing costumes with her?' he added pointedly.

Emily frantically cast around for a reason that might be credible. 'Maybe she had to abandon them to get away from Jacques. I left quite a lot of my things behind on the yacht…'

'In *your* bid to escape.'

'Yes.'

'To escape what, Miss Ross?' he asked silkily. 'You must admit Arnault has kept to the bargain you made with him, bringing you to Zanzibar, as agreed.'

'Not to the public harbour at Stone Town, monsieur.'

'This private harbour is along the way. He was on course to Stone Town.'

'I couldn't trust him to take me there. After doing his

business at this location, he might have set sail for Madagascar, keeping me on as his crew.'

'So you chose to commit yourself to a formidable swim in unknown waters, then brave facing a mangrove swamp in the darkness. This is the act of a desperate person, Miss Ross.'

'A determined person,' she corrected, though she was beginning to feel deeply desperate in the face of this prolonged cross-examination.

'The kind of desperate person who will do anything to avoid facing prison,' he went on with an air of ruthless logic. 'A guilty person…'

'I haven't done anything wrong!' she yelled, cracking under the pressure of his disbelief in her testimony. 'I promised my sister I'd be in Stone Town for her and I wasn't sure Jacques would take me there.'

'Your sister. Who is your sister?'

'Who are *you*?' she whipped back, so frustrated by his incessant questioning of *her* position, the urge to attack *his* completely dismissed caution. 'My sister and I have important private business. I'm not going to tell a stranger what it is.'

Her defiant stance earned a glance that told her she was being utterly ridiculous in his opinion, but Emily didn't care. She wanted some answers, too.

'You are addressing Sheikh Zageo bin Sultan Al Farrahn,' he stated loftily.

A sheikh! Or was it a Sultan? He'd spoken both titles and either one made instant sense of this amazing place. But did he have any jurisdiction here?

'I thought Sultan rule was long gone from Zanzibar and the island is now under the government of Tanzania,' she threw back at him.

'While it has become part of Tanzania, Zanzibar maintains its own government,' he sharply corrected her. 'And I command considerable respect and influence here. Instead of fighting me, Miss Ross, you would do well in these circumstances to seek my favour.'

'And what does seeking your favour entail?'

Fiery contempt blazed from her eyes. Her nerves were wound up so tightly, she felt like a compressed spring about to explode from its compression. If he dared suggest a *sexual* favour…if he dared even lower his gaze to survey her curves again…Emily knew she'd completely lose it and start fighting like a feral cat.

Fortunately she was not dealing with a stupid man. 'Perhaps you need time to consider your position, Miss Ross,' he said in a reasoning tone. 'Time to appreciate the importance of giving appropriate information so you can be helped.'

Emily's mind slid from attack mode and groped towards wondering if she'd taken a self-defeating angle throughout this interview.

Her questioner lifted his arms into a wide, open-handed gesture. 'Let us continue this conversation when you are feeling more comfortable. A warm bath, a change of clothes, some refreshment…'

She almost sagged at the heavenly thought.

'I'll have my men escort you to the women's quarters.' Right at this moment, Emily didn't care if the women's quarters was a harem full of wives and concubines. It would be good to be amongst *females* again, great to sink into a warm bath and get cleaned up, and a huge relief to be dressed in clothes that provided some sense of protection from the far too *male* gaze of Sheikh Zageo bin Sultan Al Farrahn.

CHAPTER THREE

ZAGEO glanced over the contents of the waterproof bag, now emptied onto a side table in his private sitting room and divided into categories for his perusal. He picked up the passport. If it was a genuine document, Emily Ross was an Australian citizen, born in Cairns. Her date of birth placed her as currently twenty-eight years old.

'You have looked up this place…Cairns?' he asked his highly reliable aide-de-camp, Abdul Haji.

'A city on the east coast of far north Queensland, which is the second largest state in Australia,' Abdul informed, once again proving his efficiency in supplying whatever Zageo did or might require. 'The paper certifying Miss Ross as a diving instructor,' he went on, gesturing to a sheaf of documents on the table, 'is attached to various references by employers who have apparently used her services, catering for tourists at The Great Barrier Reef. They are not immediately checkable because of the different time zone, but in a few hours…'

Zageo picked up the papers. The certificate was

dated six years ago so Emily Ross had apparently been plying this profession since she was twenty-two. 'The resort on the Red Sea where Arnault supposedly picked up this woman…'

'Is renowned for its diving around magnificent coral reefs,' Abdul instantly slid in. 'However, it also employs belly-dancers for nightly entertainment.'

Zageo flashed him a sardonic smile. 'We will soon see if that picture fits.' He waved to the meagre bundle of clothes. 'This appears to be survival kit only.'

'One can easily replenish lost clothes by purchasing them very cheaply at the markets.'

Zageo picked up a small bundle of American dollars and flicked through them to check their value. 'There's not much cash money here.'

'True. No doubt Miss Ross was counting on using her credit card.'

Which was also laid out on the table—a Visa card, acceptable currency in most hotels. All the same, transactions and movements could be traced from a credit card, which didn't exactly tally with criminal activities.

'Surely there should be more ready cash if she is involved in the drug-running,' Zageo observed.

Abdul shrugged. 'We have no direct evidence of her complicity. I am inclined to believe she did make a deal with Arnault—free passage to wherever she wanted to go in return for crewing on his yacht…'

'And sharing his bunk.'

The cynical deduction evoked a frown that weighed

other factors. 'Curiously the search of Arnault's yacht indicated separate sleeping quarters.'

'Perhaps the man snores.'

'There does not appear to be any love lost between them,' Abdul pointed out. 'Arnault is eager to trade Miss Ross for his freedom and…'

'She jumps overboard rather than be caught with him. As you say, no love lost between them but sex can certainly be used as a currency by both parties.'

'Then why would Miss Ross not use her very blatant sex appeal to win your favour?'

It was a good question.

In fact, she should have done. It was what Zageo was used to from the women he'd met in western society. For Emily Ross to be an exception to the rule made no sense whatsoever. It was a totally perverse situation for her to look furious at his taking note of her feminine attributes, and to try blocking his appreciation of the perfectly proportioned curves by folding her arms. Women who wanted to win his interest invariably flaunted every charming asset they had. It was the oldest currency in the world for getting where they wanted to be. So why was Emily Ross denying it?

By her own admission she was not an innocent virgin.

Nor was she too young to know the score when it came to dealings between men and women.

Many things about this woman did not add up to a logical answer. The way she had spoken to him— actually daring to challenge him—had verged on disrespect, yet there had been a quick and lively intelligence behind everything she'd said. Those amazingly vivid blue eyes could have played flirtatious games with him, but no, they had burned with the strongly defiant sense of her own individuality, denying *him* any power over her, showing contempt for his authority.

'That woman needs to be put in her place,' Zageo muttered, determined to do it before the night was very much older.

Abdul's brow furrowed into another frown of uncertainty. He started stroking his beard, a sure sign of some perturbation of mind. 'If she *is* Australian…'

'Yes?' Zageo prompted impatiently.

'Perhaps it is because they are from a country which is detached from everywhere else…I have found Australians to be strangely independent in how they think and act. They are not from an authoritarian society and they think they have the right to question anything. In fact, those who have been in our employ at Dubai have bluntly stated we will get a better result if we let them perform in their own way.'

Zageo waved dismissively. 'You are talking of men. Men who have gained some eminence in their fields.'

'Yes, but I'm thinking this may be an endemic attitude amongst both men and women from Australia.'

'You are advising me that this woman may not be in the habit of bowing to any authority?'

Abdul grimaced an apologetic appeal to soften any offence as he explained, 'I'm saying Miss Ross may not have the mindset to bend to your will. It is merely something to be considered when taking in the whole.'

'Thank you, Abdul. I will give more thought to the problem of Miss Ross. However, until such time as you have checked the references from her previous employers, we will pursue the course I have laid down. Please ensure that my instructions are followed.'

Abdul bowed his way out.

His aide always understood authority.

To Zageo's mind it was utterly intolerable for Emily Ross not to bend to his will. At the very least the woman was guilty of trespassing. It was unreasonable of her to keep defying all he stood for.

She had to bend.

He would make her bend!

Emily's bikini had been taken away while she was relaxing in a luxurious spa bath, enjoying the warm bursts of water on tired, stiff muscles and the aromatic mixture of lavender and sandalwood oils rising out of the bubbles. She'd been invited to wear a wraparound silk robe during the subsequent pampering—a manicure and pedicure while her hair was shampooed and blow-dried. Five star service in these women's quarters, Emily thought, until it came time to discard the robe and dress for her next meeting with the sheikh.

She was ushered into a sumptuous bedroom where there was only one outfit on offer. It had not come from her waterproof bag. It had not come from the luggage she'd chosen to leave behind on the yacht. It did not belong to her but Emily knew instantly what it represented. Sheikh Zageo bin Sultan Al Farrahn wanted to see how well she fitted the contentious belly-dancing role. Without a doubt this was one of the costumes he'd accused her of owning.

The skirt seemed to be a concoction of chiffon scarves with colours ranging from deep violet, through many shades of blue to turquoise. These layers were attached to a wide hip band encrusted with royal-blue and gold and silver sequins with a border of dangling gold medallions. Violet lycra hipster panties came with the skirt. The cups and straps of the accompanying turquoise bra were also exotically patterned with sequins and beads.

Clearly this was not a cheap dress-up outfit.

It was an intricably fashioned professional costume.

Emily felt a twinge of concern for the woman to whom it did belong. What had happened to her? What was the story behind the storage of these specialty clothes on the yacht?

'I can't wear that,' she protested to Heba, the oldest of the attendants who'd been looking after her. 'It's not mine,' she insisted.

'I have been instructed it is for you,' came the inarguable reply. 'His Excellency, the sheikh, has commanded that you wear it. There is no other choice.'

Emily gritted her teeth. Clearly His Excellency's word was law in this household. He'd allowed her the leeway of cleaning up and feeling more comfortable, although most probably this indulgence was a premeditated softening up process and Emily was highly suspicious of the motive behind it.

Was the sexual trade-off still being considered?

Had she just been prepared for the sheikh's bed?

It had been so easy to accept all the pampering but now came the crunch!

She could either dig in her heels and remain naked under the flimsy and all too revealing silk robe—not a good option—or don the belly-dancing costume which was probably less sexually provocative and would definitely leave her less physically accessible.

Given there would be no avoiding facing the sheikh again tonight—he'd have her hauled into his presence if she tried disobeying his instructions—Heba was right. No choice. It had to be the belly-dancing costume.

Emily quelled a flood of futile rebellion and grudgingly accepted the inevitable, thinking that with any luck, these blatantly sexy clothes wouldn't fit and *that* would show him she'd been telling the truth.

Naturally the lycra panties proved nothing, stretching to accommodate her derriere. No problem. Annoyingly the skirt sat snugly on the curve of her hips—not too loose, not too tight. Emily eyed the bra balefully as she discarded the silk robe. It looked about right, but hopefully it wouldn't comfortably reach around her back.

To her intense frustration, the straps were perfectly positioned for her shape, the hooks and eyes met with no trouble at all, and the wired cups designed to uplift breasts and emphasise cleavage made her look so voluptuous it was positively embarrassing. Okay, her breasts were not small, but they weren't this *prominent*.

The belly-dancing costume actually made her feel more self-conscious of her body than the swamp-soiled bikini which had been whisked away the moment she'd discarded it to step into the spa bath. The skimpy two-piece had been a far more natural thing for her to wear. It hadn't been exotic and erotic, aimed at titillating a man's mind. It had simply been an off-the-peg garment for swimming.

However, there was no point in asking for it back.

Heba had her orders and clearly disobeying the sheikh was unthinkable.

Emily argued to herself that although she might *feel* caught up in a scene from *The Arabian Nights*, it couldn't be true, not in today's world. Even Heba was now using a very modern slimline mobile phone, un-doubtedly reporting the state of play.

This forcing her to wear the belly-dancing costume had to be a pressure tactic, wanting her to feel more ex-posed, more vulnerable in the next interview about her activities. It couldn't have anything to do with a sexual trade-off. Not really.

Two security guards and a bearded man whom they clearly regarded as a higher authority arrived to escort her elsewhere. The women's quarters were on the sec-ond floor. Emily expected to be taken all the way down to the opulent atrium but she was led to a door on the first floor, which instantly evoked a wild wave of ap-prehension. At least the hugely open atrium had been like a public arena, overlooked by anyone on the ground or upper floors. She hoped, quite desperately, that some kind of official office was behind this door.

It wasn't.

The bearded man ushered her into what was undoubtedly a private sitting room, richly furnished and sensually seductive with its many cushioned couches surrounding a low circular table which held a tempting display of food and drink. It was occupied by only one person who instantly proceeded to dismiss her usher.

'Thank you, Abdul.'

The bearded man backed out of the room and closed the door, leaving Emily absolutely alone with a sheikh who apparently believed the only law that had to be respected was his own!

He strolled forward, intent on gaining an unencumbered view of her from head to foot—front view, side view and back view—in the costume he'd chosen for her to wear. Emily gritted her teeth and stood as still as a statue, determined not to betray her inner quaking and hoping that with her head held high, she looked as though she disdained any interpretation he took from how well the skirt and bra fitted her.

He moved behind her. Her spine crawled with an awareness of how close he was. Within an arm's reach. And he did not move on. His out-of-sight stillness played havoc with her pulse, making her temples throb with acute anxiety. What was he doing? What was he thinking? Was she imagining it or had he touched her hair, sliding fingers around a tress, lifting it away from the rest?

'You must fetch a very high price…as a dancer.'

The comment was spoken slowly, consideringly, his voice thick with a sensuality that raised goose-bumps all over her skin.

Emily swallowed hard to work some moisture into a very dry mouth. Her inner agitation had bolted beyond any control. Remaining still was beyond her. She swung around, catching sight of a swathe of her hair sliding out between the thumb and fingers of a hand that had been raised to his mouth. Or nose. The idea of him taking the intimate liberty of tasting it, smelling it, created total havoc in Emily's mind.

'You're making a big mistake about me,' she cried, struggling to find some defence to how he was making her feel.

'That was meant as a compliment, Miss Ross,' he answered, his mouth still curved in a look of sensual pleasure. 'There is no need for you to bristle.'

He didn't have the right to touch her without her permission. Emily wanted to say so but she sensed he would only laugh at the objection. Right now he had the power to do anything he wanted with her. All she could do was try to change his view of who and what she was.

'It sounded as though you thought I was a…a call-girl,' she protested.

His smile tilted with irony. 'I think it more a case of your choosing whom you'll take as a lover…as it suits you.'

Emily wasn't sure she liked the sound of that, either. She had the weird sensation of being silently enticed to

choose *him* as her next lover. Or was he setting a test—
a trap—for her?

'Come—' he waved her forward to one of the
couches close to the circular table '—you must be hungry after the rigours of your escape from Jacques
Arnault.'

Her stomach was empty—so empty it kept convuls-
ing with nervous energy. 'Does this mean you believe
I was escaping from him and not involved in the drug-
running?' she asked, not yet ready to take a step in any
direction.

He swept her an open-handed, graceful gesture.
'Until we reach a time and place of complete enlightenment, I would prefer you to consider yourself more
my guest than my prisoner.'

'You mean you *are* actually checking me out,' Emily
pursued the point, hoping for some sense of relief from
his false assumptions about her.

'Different time zones do not permit that process at
the moment but rest assured nothing will be taken for
granted. In the meantime…'

'I am hungry,' she admitted, thinking she'd feel safer
sitting down, safer keeping her mouth busy with eating
if she could make her stomach cooperate with an intake
of food.

Again he waved her forward. 'Please…seat yourself comfortably, relax, and help yourself to whatever
you'd like.'

No way in the world could she ever relax in this
man's company, but putting a table between them

seemed like a good defensive move. 'Thank you,' she said, forcing her feet to walk slowly, waiting for him to indicate where he would sit so she could settle as far away from him as possible.

Apparently he wanted to be face-to-face with her so she didn't have to manoeuvre for a position opposite to his. He took it himself. Nevertheless, there was still a disturbing sense of intimacy, just in their being seated at the same table. The couches around it were curved, linking with each other so there was no real sense of separation.

'What would you like to drink?' he asked, as though she truly were a guest. 'You have a choice of mango, pineapple and hibiscus juices, coconut milk…'

'Hibiscus juice?' She'd heard of the flower but hadn't known a drink could be made from it.

'Sweet, light and refreshing.' He reached for a jug of hand-painted pottery depicting a red hibiscus. 'Want to try it?'

'No, thanks. I've always loved mango.' Which she was long familiar with since it was such a prolific fruit tree around her home city of Cairns.

His dark eyes danced with mocking amusement over her suspicious refusal of the hibiscus jug. 'Where has your adventurous spirit gone, Miss Ross?'

The light taunt goaded her into shooting some straight truth right back at him. 'I feel like having some familiar comfort right now, Your Excellency.'

He picked up another pottery jug and poured mango juice into a beautiful crystal goblet. 'The familiar is safe,' he observed, a glittering challenge in his eyes as he replaced the jug and watched her pick up the goblet. 'A woman who plays safe would never have boarded Arnault's yacht. She would have taken a far more conventional, more protected route to Zanzibar.'

Emily fervently wished she had. Never more so than now. Dealing with this sheikh and his attitude towards her was undermining her self-confidence. She didn't know how to even set about *getting out of this*. Telling the truth didn't seem to be winning her anything, but what else could she do?

'I've crewed on yachts many times around the Australian coast. I was looking for a way to save the cost of plane fares.'

'You took a risk with a stranger.'

'I thought I could handle it.'

'And when you woke up and found there was no wife…how did you handle it then, Miss Ross?'

'Oh, then it came down to the rules of survival at sea. We needed each other to sail the yacht so agreements had to be reached and kept. Jacques only tried to cross the line once.' Her eyes hardened with the contempt she felt for the Frenchman. 'I think he found it too painful to repeat that particular error in judgment.'

The sheikh's mouth twitched into a sardonic little smile. 'Perhaps this contributed to Arnault's belief you were a virgin, Miss Ross, fighting for your virtue.'

She rolled her eyes. 'One doesn't have to be a virgin to not want a scumbag sharing your bed.'

'A scumbag…'

'The lowest of the low,' she drily explained.

'Ah!' One eyebrow arched in wicked challenge. 'And what of the highest of the high, Miss Ross? Where does your measure start for a man to be accepted into your bed?'

The highest of the high...

Emily's heart catapulted around her chest.

He was speaking of himself. Had to be. Which made this question far too dangerous to answer. If he actually did want to be accepted into her bed...the speculative look in his eyes was making her toes curl.

Emily quickly reached out to pick up some tasty tidbit from the table to stuff in her mouth.

Eating was safe.

Speaking was dangerous.

She was suddenly heart-thumpingly sure that a desire for sexual satisfaction was more on Sheikh Zageo bin Sultan Al Farrahn's mind than a desire for truth, and what he wanted from her was capitulation, vindicating everything he thought about her.

No way.

Never, she thought fiercely.

But what if he kept her here until she did give him the satisfaction he expected from her? She might never get to Stone Town for the meeting with her sister!

CHAPTER FOUR

ZAGEO watched Emily Ross eat. The consumption of an array of finger food was done with such single-minded focus, she could well have been absolutely alone in the room. *He* rated no visible attention whatsoever.

In any other woman's company he would find this behaviour unforgivably rude. In fact, he couldn't recall such a situation ever happening before. Emily Ross was proving to be an intriguing enigma on many levels, and perversely enough, her constantly challenging attitude was exciting more than just an intellectual interest in her. Mind-games with a woman were always sexy.

He suspected if he made some comment about her concentration on the food, she would lift those incredibly vivid blue eyes and state very reasonably, 'You invited me to help myself. Do you now have some problem with me doing it?'

What reply could he make to that without sounding *un*reasonable?

The plain truth was he felt peeved by her refusal to

show more awareness of him. It pricked his male ego. But he could wait. Time was on his side. Let her satisfy this hunger. If she was using it as an evasive tactic, it would come to an end soon enough and she'd be forced to acknowledge him again.

Besides, the Frenchman had not been wrong in his assessment of this woman's physical attractions. She was intensely watchable. Her hair alone was a visual delight—not just one block of colour but an intriguing meld of many variations in shades of blond and copper. The description of 'strawberry-blonde' had suggested red hair and pale skin, but there was more of an overall warm glow in Emily Ross's colouring. Her skin did not have the fairness that freckled. It was lightly tanned to a golden-honey shade.

Copper and gold, he thought. A woman of the sun with eyes the colour of a clear, sun-kissed sky. But her body belonged to Mother Earth, the fullness of her breasts and the width of her hips promising an easy fertility and a natural ability to nurture that Zageo was finding extremely appealing.

Perhaps it was the contrast to Veronique's chic model thinness that had him so…fascinated…by this woman's more opulent femininity. The lavish untamed hair denied any skilful styling by a fashionable hairdresser. The lavish flesh of her body—not fat, just well covered, superbly covered—allowed no bones to protrude anywhere, and would undoubtedly provide a soft cushioning for anyone lying with her—man or child.

She was a creature of nature, not the creation of diet

and designer wear, and Zageo found himself wanting to lie with her, wanting to sink into her softness and wanting to feel her heat envelop him and suck him in to the deepest part of her where secrets melted and intimacy reigned. That was when she would surrender to him. Utterly and completely.

Zageo relished the thought of Emily Ross's ultimate submission as he watched her eat. He was inclined to believe the Frenchman had not managed to get that satisfaction from her. Arnault's sexual frustration would have primed his readiness to try selling her on, demonstrating a total lack of perception about Zageo's character and the woman's. Emily Ross was of the mettle to play her own game by her own rules.

Nevertheless, Zageo had no doubt she could be bought, just like everyone else.

It was always a matter of striking the right trade.

The challenge was in finding out what buttons to press for the door of opportunity to open.

'Where were you aiming to meet your sister in Stone Town?' he asked.

Important private business—if Emily Ross had spoken the truth about her motive for coming to Zanzibar—invariably provided leverage.

Emily chewed over that question as she finished a tasty egg and asparagus tartlet and sipped some more mango juice. She didn't like the past tense he'd used, suggesting she wasn't going to be allowed to keep her appointment with Hannah.

Her gaze targeted his, projecting very direct intent. 'I still aim to meet her. She's counting on my meeting her. I left the yacht and swam for it because I didn't want to let my sister down.'

'Is she in trouble?'

The quick injection of concern almost tripped Emily into spilling her own worries about Hannah's situation. Caution clamped onto her tongue before it ran loose with information that was better kept private. Being an Australian, she was in the habit of assuming the world around her was safe unless it was proved otherwise. She had just been learning—the hard way—that she trusted too easily. Blithely believing that most people were of goodwill could land her in very nasty places.

'It's just a family meeting. I said I'd come. She'll be expecting me,' Emily stated, trying to sound matter-of-fact rather than anxious.

'Miss Ross, if I am to believe you were not in league with Arnault and his drug-running…' He paused to give emphasis to his line of argument. 'If I am to believe in your determination to meet your sister in Stone Town…there must be a designated place—be it hotel, shop, or private residence—and a name that can be checked there, giving credence to your story.'

Okay, she could see there was a credibility gap here that had to be crossed or her guest/prisoner status would remain as long as the sheikh cared to keep it in place. On the other hand, from the way he'd been eyeing her over, Emily had the distinctly uneasy feeling that not even credibility would earn her release from his custody. Still, she had to offer some proof that she was on a completely separate mission to Jacques Arnault's.

'The Salamander Inn. I don't know if Hannah has booked ahead. Unlikely, I'd think, since she was unsure of when she'd make it to Zanzibar. But that's our meeting place.'

'The Salamander Inn is a boutique hotel. It offers the best and coincidentally the most expensive accommodation of all the hotels on this island. I know this.' He smiled with an arrogance that somehow implied she'd just been very stupid. 'I own it.'

Oh, great! The chance of escaping from this man anywhere on Zanzibar looked increasingly dim!

'Fine!' she said on an exasperated sigh. 'Then you can easily check if Hannah has arrived or not.'

'Her full name?'

'Hannah Coleman.'

'Not Ross?'

'Coleman is her married name.'

'So your sister is not likely to book under the family name of Ross?'

'Hardly. Ross is *my* married name.'

That information ripped him out of his languid pose against the heaps of satin cushions on his couch. His body jerked forward, his loose robes suddenly pasted to a tautly muscled physique that seemed to bristle with assault readiness. Yet he spoke with a soft silky contempt which crawled straight under Emily's skin, priming her into retaliation mode.

'Where is your husband, Madame Ross?'

'His ashes were thrown to a breeze out at sea…as he'd once said he'd prefer to being buried,' Emily grated out, hanging firmly to being matter-of-fact so that she wasn't embarrassed by one of the waves of grief which could still sweep up and overwhelm her when she thought of Brian's death.

They'd been school sweethearts, rarely parted during all the years they'd spent sharing almost everything in each other's company. Then to have him taken from her so abruptly…being left behind…alone…cheated of a future together… *No, no, no, don't go there, Emily!*

She concentrated on watching her antagonist digest the news of her widowhood, the withdrawal of all expression from his face, the slow emergence of more sympathetic inquiry in his dynamic dark eyes.

'How long ago?' he asked quietly.

'About two years.'

'He was young?'

'Two years older than me.'

'How did he die?'

'Brian was with a rescue team during a cyclone.' She grimaced. 'He died trying to save an old lady's pet dog. A panel of flying roof hit him.'

'A brave man then,' came the thoughtful observation.

She managed an ironic smile. 'I don't think fear ever had any influence on Brian's actions. He just did whatever he set out to do. We used to go adventuring a lot, working our way around Australia.'

'You do not have children?'

She shook her head. 'We weren't ready to settle

down with a family. In fact, we were getting ready to set off on a world trip…'

'When the cyclone happened,' he finished for her.

'Yes,' she muttered, frowning at the realisation that she'd spoken more of Brian in the past two minutes than in the entire two years since her departure from Australia.

You have to move on, she'd told herself, and move on she had, a long slow trip across Asia, more or less going wherever the wind blew her on her travels, not wanting to face making any long-term decisions about her life—a life without the man who'd always coloured it.

She'd attached herself to other groups of people from time to time, working with them, listening to their experiences, soaking up interesting pieces of information, but what was highly personal and private to her had remained in her own head and heart.

So why had she opened up to this man?

Her mind zapped back the answer in no time flat.

Because *he* was getting to her in a highly primitive male/female way and she'd instinctively brought up the one man she'd loved as a shield against these unwelcome feelings. Her marriage to Brian was a defence against other things, as well, like the idea she was a belly-dancer with indulgent sugar-daddies on the side.

She was, in fact, a perfectly respectable widow who hadn't even been tempted into a sexual dalliance by the many gorgeous eye-candy guys who'd offered to share their beds and bodies while they were ships passing on their separate journeys. Sex without emotional involvement hadn't appealed, and it didn't appeal now, either, she fiercely told herself, willing her body to stop responding in this embarrassingly *animal* fashion to a very foreign sheikh who wanted to treat her as a whore.

Having worked up a head of defensive steam, Emily lifted her gaze to the man in the ruling seat and noted that his disturbingly handsome head was cocked to one side as though viewing her from an angle he hadn't considered before, and the heart-thumping power of those brilliant dark eyes was thankfully narrowed into thoughtful slits.

'So what is *your* marital status?' she bluntly demanded.

His head snapped upright, eyes opening wide with a flash of astonishment at her temerity. 'I beg your pardon?'

'Fair's fair!' Emily argued. 'If you have the right to ask about mine, I have just as much right to ask about yours.'

If he had a string of wives and a bevy of concubines, perhaps he would cease to be so attractive!

His face clearly said she was being incredibly impertinent but Emily didn't care. 'After all, what do I know about you?' she pointed out. 'I'll accept you're Sheikh Zageo…whatever…whatever…and you own this place as well as The Salamander Inn, which obviously means you're terribly wealthy and probably influential, but—'

'Zageo bin Sultan Al Farrahn,' he broke in haughtily, supplying all the names she'd forgotten in her current fraught state.

'Right! Quite a mouthful to remember,' she excused. 'Though if it's a big issue to you, I'll try to hold it in my mind.'

'Rather than test your mind too far,' he drawled in a mocking tone that once more raised Emily's hackles. 'You may call me Zageo in my private rooms.'

'Well, thank you very much. It was really sticking in my craw, having to address you as Your Excellency,' she tossed at him. 'I mean honestly... how do you keep a straight face when people call you that? Though I suppose if you actually believe it fits you...' She paused to look at him in arch inquiry, then testingly ask, 'Do you consider yourself totally excellent?'

His jawline tightened. Emily sensed that pride was warring with his own intelligence which had to concede the presence of a few little flaws. No man—nor woman—was perfect.

'It is simply the customary form of address to any sheikh in my culture,' he stated tersely. 'I doubt Her Majesty, the queen of England, considers herself majestic. Nor think herself the highest of the high when addressed as Your Highness.'

'Okay. Point made,' Emily granted, smiling to show she hadn't meant to give any offence, though secretly she felt very pleased at levelling the playing field, if only a little bit. 'If I'm allowed to call you Zageo, you needn't keep on with Miss Ross. Emily will do just fine. It's actually what I'm more used to. We're not big on titles back home in Australia.'

And he needn't think she was overly impressed by his!

'Thank you, Emily.'

He smiled, instantly driving her mind into a jangling loop that screamed *Danger! Danger! Danger!* He'd just made her name sound like an intimate caress, sending a sensual little shiver down her spine. As for his smile…it was definitely projecting a pleasurable triumph in having won this concession from her, interpreting it as a dropping of hostility and bringing a much closer meeting ground between them.

She had a mental image of him storming the ramparts of her castle and it seemed like a good idea to pull up the drawbridge and shut the gate. 'So let's get back to *your* marital status,' she said, needing back-up support to hold the barriers in place.

'I have not yet taken a wife,' Zageo answered, undermining Emily's defensive plan.

Feeling decidedly miffed by this, she remarked, 'I thought sheikhs could take as many wives as they liked. You're a late starter aren't you?'

'I believe the right choice of wife in any culture deserves deep and serious consideration, given the intention of a lifelong commitment and the resulting alliance with another family.'

'Nothing to do with love, of course,' she tossed off flippantly.

'On the contrary, I have observed that compatibility tends to breed a more lasting love than the rather fickle chemistry of *being in love*.'

She pounced on what seemed like a beacon of relief from any sexual pressure from him. 'So you don't think giving in to chemistry is a good idea.'

'It is not something I would base a marriage on, Emily, but for a time of pure pleasure—' his eyes positively glittered with white-hot sexual invitation '—I think giving in to chemistry is a very sweet and satisfying self-indulgence, to be treasured as something uniquely special to the man and woman involved.'

Emily had to suck in a quick breath to stop an imminent meltdown in her bones, brain and other body parts she didn't want to think about. 'I take it you're not a virgin then,' she shot at him, mocking the value that had apparently been put on *her* virginity.

At least it temporarily interrupted the bolt of heat from his eyes, making him blink, then triggering a rippling peal of laughter, lessening the scary tension in the room and leaving Emily feeling slightly safer.

'I have not foresworn the pleasures of the flesh…no,' he eventually drawled, his eyes dancing an all too overt anticipation of pleasures *she* might provide, which did away with any sense of relaxation.

Emily drew in a deep breath and expelled it in a long, slow sigh, desperate to reduce the seesawing inner apprehension which made thinking nimbly very difficult. She felt stripped of any clothing armour and he'd just ripped off the mental armour she'd tried to put in place. Somehow she had to keep her mind at battle readiness because the fight for freedom would probably be lost if she let herself be distracted by this man's insidious promise of pleasures, which his eyes said were hers for the taking if she co-operated with what he wanted.

The big problem was he was the kind of man who'd tempt any woman into wondering how it might be with him…if, indeed, he would deliver amazing pleasure. Probably it was *The Arabian Nights* thing again, messing with her mind, making her think of Omar Khayyam's poetry expressing regret for the fleeting sweetness of life and love, which, in turn, tapped into the lingering emptiness of missing Brian, all contributing to her feeling of *why not experience this man*?

A harsh strain of common sense insisted it would compromise her whole situation if she did. 'I have to be here for Hannah,' she muttered, savagely reminding herself of her prime motivation.

'There cannot be any urgency about this meeting with your sister or you would not have chosen to come by yacht,' Zageo pointed out.

'Even by sailing, I figured I'd make it here by about the same time as Hannah. And I preferred to save my money.'

His mouth curled into a mocking little smile. 'Staying at The Salamander Inn does not equate with *saving money*, Emily.'

He was still doubting her story.

'I didn't say *I* was going to stay there,' she reminded him.

'Where did you plan to stay?'

'If Hannah wasn't here already, I intended to find a place that suited my budget while I waited for her.'

'Then you should have no problem with accepting my hospitality while you wait for your sister's arrival in Zanzibar,' he said silkily. 'That would undoubtedly suit your budget best. No cost whatsoever.'

'Oh, right!' Emily mocked back before she could stop her tongue from cutting loose on him. 'And I suppose you'll expect me to belly-dance for you every night!'

His elegant hands performed their graceful invitational gesture. 'If you feel you should recompense me in some way, by all means…'

'What if Hannah is at the inn already?' Emily cut in, hating the sense of being helplessly cornered, and feeling that Sheikh Zageo bin Sultan Al Farrahn was enjoying himself far too much at her expense!

'That can be checked immediately.'

He leaned forward and picked up a mobile telephone from the table. The modern means of communication again struck Emily as odd in this setting but the evidence of its use all around the palace assured her that life in the twenty-first century was not excluded here. Unfortunately most of the one-sided conversation she subsequently listened to was not in English. Of all the words spoken, only the name, Hannah Coleman, was recognisable.

Emily literally sat on the edge of her seat as she waited, hoping for news that would validate her story, as well as assure her of Hannah's safe arrival. 'Well?' she prompted anxiously, once the call connection had been ended.

The dark eyes targeted hers with riveting intensity. 'Your sister is not at the inn. Nor has there been a booking in her name.'

Disappointment warred with doubt as to the truth of what she was being told. 'How do I know you're not lying?' burst from her tongue.

His face tightened forbiddingly. 'Why would I lie?'

Even to her overstrained mind, *to get me into your bed* sounded absurd, given his extraordinary good looks and incredibly wealthy resources.

Zageo's dark eyes blazed with angry suspicion as he pointed out, 'It is you, Emily Ross, who has cause to concoct many lies in order to paint yourself as an innocent victim.'

'I swear to you on any amount of bibles or Korans or whatever carries weight in both our worlds, I've told you nothing but the truth.'

One black eyebrow arched in sceptical challenge. 'Where is your sister coming from?'

'Zimbabwe.' Realising she now had to explain more, Emily offered, 'You must know about the political problems in that country. It's world news. Everyone knows. Hannah's husband is trying to hang onto his farm, but he wants her and the children out while he…'

'Children?'

'They have two young daughters. The plan was for Hannah to bring them by road into Botswana when they thought it was safe enough for her to do so, then…' A helpful link suddenly leapt into Emily's mind. 'Hannah and her husband, Malcolm, spent a vacation at The

Salamander Inn five years ago. That's why she picked it as a meeting place. She knew it and thought it was somewhere safe for both of us to get to. Since you own the inn, surely you can have a check run on the records…'

'Not at this time of night.'

'Then first thing tomorrow morning.' Emily jumped to her feet, seeing a chance to end this highly unsettling encounter with him. 'In fact, by tomorrow morning I'm sure you have the power and facilities to have lots of things about me checked, so talking any more right now is really inefficient, isn't it? I'm terribly tired and if you'd just have me taken back to the women's quarters, I'm very happy to accept your hospitality for the night and…'

He rose from his couch, choking off Emily's speech with the formidable force of energy that rose with him. For several fraught moments, his gaze locked onto hers, telegraphing a strong and ruthless promise that if she was playing him for a fool she would pay for it.

Dearly.

But he did dismiss her from his presence.

'Until tomorrow morning,' he said in sardonic agreement with her timeline.

Pretend as she might about accepting an offer of hospitality for tonight, Emily found nothing remotely hospitable about the security guards who escorted her back to the women's quarters.

She was not Sheikh Zageo bin Sultan Al Farrahn's guest.

She was his prisoner.

CHAPTER FIVE

ZAGEO paced around his sitting room, incensed by the outrageous impertinence of Emily Ross, taking her leave of him as though she had every right to do as she pleased. This woman, who had to know she was a trespasser on his goodwill, had treated him in the same intolerable manner as Veronique. Which reminded him...

With a heightened sense of deadly purpose he moved to pick up the telephone and call the Paris apartment. He had bought it to accommodate the relationship with Veronique and she had recently taken to using it as her main residence. Zageo decided it would be a suitable parting gift as he waited impatiently for her to come on line.

'Ah, *cheri*! What a lovely surprise,' she responded with a gush of pleasure when he announced himself. 'Are you missing me?'

If she wanted some proof of her pulling power she was testing the wrong man. 'Veronique, we are at an end, you and I,' he stated matter-of-factly.

'What?' Shock. Then anxiety. 'What do you mean, Zageo?'

'I mean our relationship has run its course. You were happy to remain in Paris…and I now find myself attracted to another woman.'

'You are leaving *me* for another woman?' she screeched into his ear.

A sobering lesson for taking him for granted.

'I will sign over the apartment to you—a memento of our time together and one I'm sure you'll appreciate.'

'I don't want the apartment without you in it,' she cried wildly. 'I want you, Zageo.'

A claim that left him completely cold. If she wanted him so much, she would be with him. Clearly Veronique had thought she could have her cake without supplying the ingredients that made it desirable for him, too. A deal was a deal and as far as Zageo was concerned, she hadn't lived up to her end of it. Nevertheless, he was prepared to be generous.

'Please have the grace to accept it's over, Veronique. There is nothing more to be gained by carrying on. It cannot serve any good purpose. I promise you will have the apartment. I'll put the legalities in train tomorrow.'

'You've found another woman?' Her voice shook with hysterical incredulity.

An unforgiveable wound to her pride?

'I'm sure you'll find another man,' he drawled, aware there were many ready to slide into the place he'd just vacated.

'You can't do this to me. I won't let you—'

'Move on, Veronique,' Zageo cut in ruthlessly. 'I have. Let us meet in future as old friends who still hold some affection for each other. As always, I wish you well.'

He ended the connection before she could pour out any further futile protests. It was far better to part with a sense of mutual respect than with a tirade of mutual grievances. He hoped Veronique would be pragmatic enough to accept what would not be changed and count herself fortunate to have profited so handsomely from their relationship. The gifted apartment in Paris would undoubtedly provide balm to wounded pride.

The burning question now was…how to deal with Emily Ross?

She was showing no signs whatsoever of bending to his will. Quite the contrary. Despite the fact she had to realise her immediate fate was in his hands and it would serve her well to win his favour, she was flouting his authority at every turn.

If Abdul was right about this kind of attitude being common amongst Australians, perhaps it was not meant to be so offensive. On the other hand, Zageo did not care to accept it from a woman. Of course, he could turn her in to the local authorities, move her straight out of his life, and that was certainly the most sensible path to take, given that he'd decided to find himself a suitable wife.

Emily Ross was a distraction from what he should be doing. On the other hand, for the duration of this business trip through Africa, he would very much enjoy having her in his bed and teaching her who was master of the situation.

Tomorrow he would know more about her.

Knowledge was power, especially when it came to dealing with people.

However, when tomorrow came, enlightenment did not come with it.

'Government offices are not open in Australia on Saturdays and Sundays,' Abdul reported. 'We cannot check a marriage certificate or a death certificate until Monday.'

More frustration!

Having finished eating his breakfast, Zageo took a long deliberate moment to savour the aroma of his Kenyan coffee, wanting at least one of his senses satisfied. Then he once again considered the challenging and highly vexing enigma of Emily Ross. Investigating her was like chasing evaporating smoke—no substance to be found anywhere.

Abdul had already informed him that the Australian employers who had written her references were no longer at the same place of business. Reef Wonderland Tours had changed management eighteen months ago and Whitsundays Diving Specialists was now a defunct company. As for the Red Sea resort where she had supposedly been working with a dive team, no-one admitted to knowing anything about her, which raised questions about what profession she had plied there since her name was not on any record books.

Had she spun a complete tissue of lies last night?

Was anything about her self-presentation genuine?

'The belly-dancing costume fitted her perfectly,' he remarked drily.

'Indeed, it did, Your Excellency,' Abdul agreed.

Zageo frowned over the form of address all his staff customarily used with him. Normally he just took *Your Excellency* for granted, barely hearing it, but in real terms the title *was* ridiculous, as that highly perverse and provocative creature had pointed out.

'The authorities have come from Stone Town to take Jacques Arnault and his Zanzibar connections into custody,' Abdul ran on when no further comment came from Zageo. 'A decision should be made whether or not to include Miss Ross in this criminal group.'

'Not.' The answer was swift and emphatic. He would feel…*defeated*…by Emily Ross if he washed his hands of her before coming to grips with who and what she really was. 'We have no absolute proof of involvement,' he added. 'I'm inclined to allow her the benefit of the doubt, given how very difficult it is to undo an injustice once it has been committed.'

'Do you wish to keep her here or set her free to go about her own business?'

'Since Miss Ross has no prearranged accommodation, I shall hold her here as my guest. At least until Monday.' He gave Abdul a look that conveyed his determination to pursue more background information. 'As to her business, clearly it is not urgent since a

Hannah Coleman has not, as yet, booked into The Salamander Inn. If, indeed, there is a sister to be met.'

'A search of the five-year-old records at the inn did turn up a Mr and Mrs M. Coleman.'

Zageo shrugged, unconvinced by a name that could belong to any number of people. 'One wonders if that is confirmation of my new guest's story or mere coincidence,' he drawled derisively. 'I think I shall amuse myself by doing a little more testing today, Abdul.'

His chief advisor and confidante took several moments to absorb and interpret this comment. He then cleared his throat and tentatively inquired, 'Has the…uh…affair with Veronique run its course, Your Excellency? Are there some…arrangements…you'd like me to make?'

'No. It's done. I made the call and the arrangements last night. The decision had nothing whatsoever to do with Miss Ross, Abdul. It was made beforehand.'

Although Emily Ross featured highly as a replacement for Veronique in his life, having completely obliterated his former mistress from his mind.

'I've given her the Paris apartment,' he went on. 'Ownership will need to be transferred into her name. You'll see to it?'

Abdul nodded. 'Speaking of names, the Coleman name *was* attached to an address in Zimbabwe. Do you wish me to make inquiries in that direction?'

'It could be fruitful. One might well ask why hasn't the sister turned up? Yes…' Zageo smiled to himself. 'Pursuing this question presents a nice little demonstration of concern for those whom Miss Ross apparently holds dear to her heart.'

A weapon in the war, he thought, feeling an extraordinary zing of anticipation in the plan he would soon put into operation.

CHAPTER SIX

EMILY had to concede that being a prisoner in this astounding place was not hard to take. Her physical needs were wonderfully pampered. She'd slept in a heavenly bed. Of course, after the bunk on the yacht, almost any normal bed would have been heavenly but the lovely soft mattress and pillows and the amazing curtain of mosquito netting that had been pulled all around the bed to protect her from any possible bites had definitely made her feel as though she was sleeping on clouds.

Then to wake up and find her own clothes restored to her—even those she'd had to leave behind on Jacques's yacht—all washed, ironed, and either hanging up or set on shelves in the dressing room adjoining the bedroom…well, surely this was evidence that her real life had been verified and everything was moving back to normal. The fears generated by the grotesque situation last night seemed rather incredible this morning.

She'd happily dressed in a favourite skirt made of a

pink, blue and green floral fabric that swirled freely around her legs—lovely and cool for what was shaping up to be a hot day on the island. A blue top with little sleeves and a scooped neckline completed what she considered a fairly modest outfit, definitely not overtly sexy, just…pretty…and feminine. If there was to be another face-to-face encounter with the sheikh, hopefully he wouldn't have any grounds for viewing her in a morally questionable light again.

Breakfast on the verandah outside her suite in the women's quarters became quite a social affair. As well as Heba serving her a very tasty array of fruit and croissants, her two other attendants from last night's grooming session, Jasmine and Soleila, fluttered around, eager to please Emily in any way they could.

A selection of magazines were brought for her to flick through as she finished the meal with absolutely divine coffee. Heba, herself, opened a copy of *Vogue* to show photographs of celebrities at some big premiere in Paris.

'See?' she pointed out proudly. 'Here he is with Veronique!'

Emily felt a weird catch in her heart as she stared at the stunningly beautiful Sheikh Zageo bin Sultan Al Farrahn in a formal black dinner suit, accompanied by the stunningly beautiful world-famous model, the highly unique Veronique, who was wearing a fabulous evening gown of floating ostrich feathers that only she could have carried off so magnificently.

This photograph was not a slice of fantasy out of *The*

Arabian Nights. It was real life on the international scene, the jet-setting, ultra-wealthy beautiful people doing what they do, connecting with each other for fabulous affairs—social and personal.

Feeling considerably flattened, Emily realised that her imagination must have been in an extremely feverish state last night, running hot with the idea of being seen as a desirable woman to this man. Why on earth would he want her when such an exotic and classy model was available to him?

'Have they been a couple of long standing?' she asked Heba.

A shrug. 'Almost two years.'

Two years comprised a fairly solid attachment. Emily now felt thoroughly confused over why the sheikh was bothering with her when she could have been simply passed along to the local authorities for them to sort out her association with Jacques Arnault. Why had he taken such a *sexual* interest in her? Was it only a titillated interest because the Frenchman had tried to trade her for his freedom?

'But Heba, Veronique did not come with him this time,' Jasmine pointed out, giving Emily an archly knowing look as though it was obvious to her who was being singled out to fill the sheikh's empty bed.

'Perhaps her professional commitments didn't allow it,' Emily reasoned, unable to feel the least bit flattered by the idea of being *taken* as a temporary replacement. Totally repulsed by it, in fact.

'This could be so,' Heba agreed. 'The sheikh will be

travelling through Africa for some months. Veronique may join him somewhere else on his tour of the Al Farrahn hotels.'

The Salamander Inn was obviously one of many such places, Emily thought, more proof of fabulous family wealth. Not that she needed it. What she did need was to plant her feet firmly on the ground and find a way to walk out of the hothouse atmosphere of this palace and get back to normal life, no matter how difficult her normal life could be at times. At least it was real, she told herself, and she knew how to deal with it, more or less.

'Am I allowed to leave?' she asked Heba. 'I need to get to Stone Town.'

'You must wait for a summons from His Excellency,' came the firm reply.

There was no budging the women from that position and without inside help, any chance of just walking out of the palace was zero. The only way down to the ground floor was by the balconies overlooking the central atrium and security guards were posted at the foot of each staircase. It was impossible, wearing her own clothes, to get past them without being seen and apprehended.

No doubt about it.

She was stuck in this gilded prison until Sheikh Zageo etc etc decided to release her from it.

As the morning wore on, Emily felt more and more on edge about being kept here at his leisure. What was happening? Why couldn't he make up his mind about her innocence in regard to Jacques's activities? When the summons finally came, she was bursting with impatience to be led to the man who ruled her current fate, her mind fizzing with persuasive arguments to win her freedom.

It wasn't acceptable to be either his prisoner or his guest. Now that she knew about his relationship with Veronique, any further offer of hospitality from him would have to be viewed as highly dubious. Besides, it was better all around to put this whole stressful episode behind her as fast as possible.

She did not expect to be escorted right out of the palace, transported to the harbour she had swum out of last night, and ferried to another boat!

Jacques's yacht was gone.

This was a sleek and very expensive looking motor cruiser.

Emily did not want to get out of the small outboard motorboat and climb up the ladder to the deck of a cruiser that was capable of whisking her right away from Zanzibar. Rebellion surged through her veins. She looked at the water. Was swimming away an option this time?

'It would be wasted effort, Emily,' came the sardonic remark from above.

Her stomach contracted at the sound of that voice. Her heart fluttered in a panicky fashion. All the prepared arguments in her mind started crumbling as they were hit by a sudden sense of futility. She knew with instinctive certainty that until this sheikh willed an end to the *hospitality* he was extending to her, there would be no end.

All the same, her natural independence would not roll over into abject submission. Her chin tilted defiantly as her gaze lifted to his. 'Why am I here?' she demanded. 'I thought you were going to have me checked out.'

'Unfortunately the weekend is not a good time for reaching sources of information.'

'When will be a good time?' she challenged, though mentally conceding that what he said was probably true.

He shrugged. 'Perhaps Monday.'

Monday. Two more days of living under a cloud and forced to endure the sheikh's company whenever he commanded it.

'Be my guest, come onboard,' he urged.

They were orders, not invitations. Emily heaved a fretful sigh as she rose to her feet and stepped up to the ladder. 'Some guest,' she darkly muttered. 'A considerate host would care about where I want to be and it's not on another boat.'

'But this is a pleasure boat which is fully crewed. No work at all for you,' he assured her in the silky tone that made her skin prickle with an acute sense of danger lurking.

'It's still on the water,' she grumbled.

'What a strange complaint from someone who is supposed to be a professional dive specialist!'

'Diving is something else,' she insisted.

'We shall see.'

There was something ominous in those words but

Emily was hopelessly distracted from pursuing that thought. He offered his hand to help steady her as she stepped down onto the deck and it was so startling to find him very informally clothed, wearing only a white T-shirt and casual shorts, she accepted it, and the strong fingers suddenly encompassing hers gave her a further jolt of physical awareness.

She tried not to look down at his bare legs, specifically his thighs, a glimpse of which had felt far too erotic for comfort. On a powerful male scale, they added immeasurably to his sex appeal, as did his taut cheeky butt when he turned to give instructions to a crew member.

In an instinctive need to get a grip on herself, Emily wriggled her hand out of his grasp and folded her arms across her rib cage. Then she ended up flushing horribly when he swung back to her and observed that her block-out body language had inadvertently pushed up her breasts.

'Relax, Emily,' he advised with a quirky little smile and wickedly challenging eyes. 'We're simply going for a ride to Pemba Island where the water is crystal clear and the coral reef provides superb diving.'

'How far away is it?' she asked sharply.

'Not far. People travel to it by ferry from Zanzibar.'

Ferry! Well, if she got marooned there, Emily reasoned, at least there was some form of public transport to get her back to Stone Town.

'Come.' He urged her towards the door leading to the cabin. 'We will sit in the saloon for the crossing.'

The saloon on this boat was a far cry from the cramped cabin on Jaques's yacht. Not only did it contain an elegant dining table that could seat ten people, the lounging area was also sumptuous; cream leather couches running along underneath the windows, plus a cosier conversational area with a grouping of chairs and sofas around a low table to allow the serving of light refreshments.

Emily chose to sit by the windows, her arm resting along the padded backrest of the couch as she looked out at the harbour Jacques had sailed into last night. She felt the vibration of the cruiser's big engines being revved up and knew they were about to power this motorboat out to sea.

Her *host* moved past her, seating himself on the same couch about a metre away but turned towards her, his arm hooking over the backrest, his hand dangling within easy reach of hers. Although she was acutely aware of his close presence, Emily resolutely ignored it, watching the mangrove swamp being left behind as the boat carved through the water towards the exit from the harbour.

'Do not be disturbed. We shall return,' Zageo assured her, apparently not insensitive to her inner tension.

'Why are you taking me with you to Pemba Island?' she asked, still not looking at him, afraid of revealing just how vulnerable he made her feel.

'The reefs around it are largely in a pristine condition, unspoilt coral gardens supporting a vast array of marine life,' he informed her. 'As a professional diver yourself, you may well have heard that this area is an underwater naturalist's dream.'

'No. I hadn't heard.'

'I am surprised,' he drawled. 'Pemba is now listed as one of the top dive spots in the world.'

The taunt over her ignorance of this fact goaded Emily into locking eyes with him. 'I didn't come to Zanzibar for diving,' she stated belligerently, resenting his forceful interruption of her personal mission. 'Why don't you just let me go to get about my own business?'

'What is there for you to do?' he retorted reasonably. 'Your sister has not yet checked in at The Salamander Inn. I have instructed the management there to notify me the moment Hannah Coleman arrives and identifies herself. In the meantime, what better way for you to spend today than taking up a superb diving opportunity?'

His logic was difficult to fault, yet undermining it was the undeniable fact she had been given no choice. 'You don't believe me, do you? You still think I'm a drug-running belly-dancer. And this—' she waved an arm at her luxurious surroundings '—is just another gilded prison.'

The hand lying close to hers on the backrest of the couch moved in a lazy dismissive gesture. 'I believe that most things reveal themselves, given enough time, Emily.' His eyes glinted a very direct challenge. 'If you are a professional diver, for example, I should have no doubt whatsoever about it after our visit to Pemba.'

'You want me to prove myself to you?'

His smile was slow in forming and caused her pulse to quicken. 'Perhaps I simply want to share a pleasure with you,' he suggested seductively, stirring a whole hornets's nest of hormones that buzzed their insistent message that he wanted more than an *underwater* pleasure with her.

Emily jumped to her feet, too agitated to remain seated beside him. 'Why are you doing this?' Her hands flapped in wild incomprehension of his motivation as she directly confronted him. 'I'm nobody to you. Just a passing blip on your radar screen. Totally insignificant. Why put your personal time into…?'

He surged to his feet, seeming to tower over her, causing her throat to close up, cutting off her ability to communicate by speech. He took her waving hands and planted them palm flat against his chest, holding them still with his, forcing them to feel the heat of his body through the thin cotton of his T-shirt, feel the strong beat of his heart, feel the rise and fall of his breathing, which all made her feel a terribly, terribly intimate connection with this man.

'An accident of fate?' he finished for her, though it wasn't what she'd meant to say.

Emily couldn't remember what she'd meant to say. She found herself staring at his mouth as it shaped more words—soft, silky words that slid into her ears and infiltrated her mind, somehow deactivating her own thought processes.

'Sometimes things happen for a reason—a time, a

place, a meeting which no one can foresee—and it is a huge mistake to deny it any significance. It may not be random factors driving the seemingly accidental collision, but forces of nature which we would do well to ride, Emily, because they were meant to be…meant to gain a result that would not be achieved otherwise.'

What result?

How could anything significant come from this… this mad attraction?

He slid her hands up to his shoulders and even though he released them, did she pluck them away from the tensile strength of the muscles supporting the breadth of those extremely masculine shoulders? No, she didn't! Her hands were stuck in self-indulgent mode, wanting to feel what he'd silently commanded her to feel.

And the mouth she was staring at was coming closer, still shaping words but she no longer heard them. Her heart was thundering in her ears. A wild wantonness gripped her mind and rippled through her entire body, urging an eagerness to experience whatever was about to come her way.

His lips brushed hers, the softest possible contact yet it started an electric tingling that begged for a continuation of the exciting sensation. Emily didn't move away from it. She closed her eyes and concentrated on her response to what was barely a kiss, yet it was sparking some volatile chemistry which was surprising, stunning, mesmerising.

Another brushing.

A slow glide of the tip of his tongue, sensually persuasive in parting her lips, caressing the soft inner tissues.

She felt him move, stepping closer to her, hands sliding around her waist, arms drawing her into a full body contact embrace. One part of her mind warned that she shouldn't be allowing this, but the clamouring need to feel and know the full extent of her response to him overrode any niggling sense of caution.

All her nerve ends seemed to be humming in vibrant anticipation of more and more stimulation. To deny the desire he stirred was impossible and she couldn't find a strong enough reason to fight it. The sheer, dizzying maleness of him called to her female instincts to revel in his strength, exult in his desire for her, savour the potency of the sexual chemistry that obliterated the differences between them—the differences that should keep them apart.

His mouth took possession of hers, no longer seductively intent, but ruthlessly confident of kissing her in whatever way he willed, smashing any inhibitions Emily might have, arousing mind-blowing excitement, inciting highly erotic passion that shot quivers of need through her entire body—a thrilling need, an aching need, a rampant all-consuming need.

She felt his fingers entangling themselves in her hair, tugging her head in whatever direction his mouth wanted to take in kissing her, felt his other hand tracing the curve of her back, reaching the pit of it, applying the pressure to mould the softness of her stomach around the hard thrust of his erection.

His sexual domination of her was so strong, Emily barely registered that she was perilously close to letting the situation reach a point of no return. She forced her mind out of its whirl of sensation long enough to consider what the outcome might be from having sex with this man.

She didn't know.

Couldn't even begin to guess.

And the sense of losing all control of her life was suddenly very frightening.

CHAPTER SEVEN

ZAGEO was so acutely attuned to the flow of mutual sexual desire between them, he instantly felt the sudden jolt of resistance that spelled imminent change. Emily's pliant body started to stiffen, muscles tightening up, shrinking from contact with him. She jerked her head back from his, shock on her face, panic in her eyes. Fight would come next, he realised, if he didn't act to soothe the fear and calm her agitation.

'Enough?' he asked, forcing his mouth into a whimsical little smile, even as his gut twisted painfully at the necessity to reclaim control of the extremely basic need she'd ignited in him.

Her lovely long throat moved convulsively as she struggled to get her thoughts in order and make a sensible reply. The vivid blue circles of her irises were diminished by huge black pupils, yet to return to normal size. She licked her lips, as though desperate to wipe the taste of his from them. But there could be no denial of her complicity in what they'd just shared. He had given her time enough to reject a kiss. She had not rejected it. Nor any other move he'd made on her up until now.

'This is not a good idea!' she pushed out emphatically, then scooped in a deep breath to deliver more oxygen to a brain which was probably feeling even more heated than his.

'On the contrary, the most beneficial existence comes from having one's mind in harmony with one's body. Mentally fighting what comes naturally is the bad idea, Emily,' he asserted.

'Right!' Another deep breath as she collected her wits, belatedly plucking her hands off his shoulders and spreading out her palms in an appeal for understanding. 'Well, just so you know, Zageo, my mind was off in la-la land and my body took a turn all on its own, which doesn't come under the heading of *harmony*!'

'And if your mind had not been in la-la land, what might it have thought?' he swiftly challenged, needing an insight into what drove her behaviour.

She eased her lower body back from his and he dropped his hands from her waist, letting her move to whatever she considered a *safe* distance.

'I'm sure you're well aware of being attractive to the opposite sex,' came the quick chiding, her eyes already deriding any protest on that score.

'You are not without attractions yourself,' he pointed out.

A tide of hot embarrassment swept up her throat and into her cheeks. 'Sometimes it's definitely better to ignore all that stuff because it's a distraction from really important things,' she argued. 'Getting personally involved with you…'

'May well be the best way of resolving the important things you speak about,' he suggested.

'No-o-o…' She shook her head vehemently as her feet backed further away. 'That's not how I conduct my life. I don't go in for using people.'

'There is nothing wrong with fair trading. If each person gives and receives something equitable…if mutual pleasure is reached…'

'I don't believe in poaching on other people's territory!' she hurled at him, fiercely defensive, her eyes flaring an accusation of unfair play.

Zageo frowned, puzzled by the offence she clearly felt. 'You gave me to understand that no man had any current claim on you,' he reminded her. 'Naturally I would have respected…'

Anger erupted. 'What about respecting the relationship you have with Veronique?'

Enlightenment dawned.

Gossip in the women's quarters.

Emily forgot about retreating further and took a belligerent stance, hands planted on her hips as she delivered a blast of scorn. 'Just because she couldn't come with you doesn't give you the right to play fast and loose with any woman who crosses your path.'

'Veronique is in Paris because being there is more attractive to her than being with me,' he drily informed.

'Our relationship has come to an end. So I am completely free, Emily, to be with any woman I choose.'

He could see her mentally floundering over the news that he had no moral obligation to Veronique. Having a strong defensive line demolished at one stroke was not easy to absorb. He wondered if her sense of morality was as sharp as she'd just indicated or had she snatched at Veronique as an excuse to evade the truth of her own desire for him?

But why did she *wish* to evade it?

'*You* choose,' she repeated, picking up the words with the air of grabbing new weapons for a further fight between them. She flung her hands up in the air. 'All the choice is yours. *I'm* not getting any choice in what's going on here. You have me kept in the women's quarters of your family palace, brought out to this boat…'

'I did not imagine your willingness to be in my embrace, Emily,' he cut in with unshakeable authority. 'As to the rest, is it not better to be under my personal protection than to be locked up in a public prison while the local authorities sort out the situation that has evolved from *your* choices?'

'At least it would have been in the process of being sorted,' she threw at him, apparently undeterred by the prospect of being forced into the company of more criminals.

'Believe me, Emily, it is best left to me to do the sorting as I have a personal interest in getting answers. However, since a choice means so much to you, I offer you one. You can come with me to Pemba Island and demonstrate how proficient you are at diving or I can instruct the captain of this vessel to take us directly to Stone Town where you can be taken into custody by local officials and rot in jail while *they* get around to checking your story in their own good time, dependent on how much paperwork is already on their desks.'

'You could just let me go,' she pressed, her whole body taut with exasperation at the limitations he was imposing on her.

'That is not an option,' Zageo answered, ruthlessly intent on keeping her with him.

'Why not?'

'I would not be doing my civic duty to release a potentially dangerous drug-runner into the community.'

'But you don't mind kissing a potentially dangerous drug-runner,' she mocked.

'It was not doing any public harm and I was prepared to take the personal risk,' he mocked straight back.

'You're not risking anything.'

'Do not speak for me, Emily. Speak for yourself. Make your choice. Do you wish me to call the captain and change our destination or do you wish to dive with me at Pemba Island? I might add that your professional referees are out of contact so there is no quick way of checking your story today. That has already been tried.'

Her long lashes dropped but not before he glimpsed a look of helpless confusion in her eyes. She heaved a long ragged sigh. 'Okay,' she finally said in a tone of reluctant resignation. 'I'll need a wetsuit. And I'll want to check the diving equipment.'

'There is a Diving Centre at Fundu Lagoon where we will drop anchor. I have directed that a diving specialist be on hand to outfit us correctly and guide us to the best viewing places around the reef.'

She nodded distractedly, her gaze flitting around the saloon and fastening on the staircase. 'Does that lead down to a…a powder room?'

'To the staterooms, each of which has an ensuite bathroom.' Aware that she was emitting frantic vibrations in a pressing need to escape him, he waved her off on her own. 'Just go down and open the first door you come to, Emily.'

'Thank you.'

She shot him a look of almost anguished relief which Zageo pondered as she hurried to the staircase and disappeared below deck.

Was it a desperate call of nature that had to be answered or a desperate need to get away by herself to reassess her position?

Zageo had to concede feeling a considerable amount of confusion himself. He'd kissed and been kissed by many women in his time. None had ever transmitted the sense of being inexperienced, innocent, virginal. It had been strangely fascinating to feel Emily Ross focusing an intense awareness on the touch and taste of his mouth, as though she'd never been kissed before, or it had been so long since she'd had the experience, she'd forgotten what it was like.

Needing to clear his own head of that tantalising impression, Zageo left the saloon and moved out to the rear deck where he could feel the sea breeze in his hair and the light spray from the boat's wake on his face. It was good to cool off. He hadn't anticipated the swift fuelling of his own desire for her. Giving in to temptation often proved a disappointment—the experience not living up to the promise. But Emily Ross…the way she'd responded…it had been *without any artfulness*!

Unless she was an unbelievably good actress, so steeped in deception it came naturally to her, Zageo could not see her fitting the frame of a belly-dancer with patrons on the side. It was far more likely that she had only known one lover—a young husband who had not been well skilled in the erotic arts. How else could those quite electric moments of stillness from her be explained? Stillness followed by a flood of chaotic excitement. It was definitely not a *knowing* response to him, more instinctive, primal, and so strong it frightened her.

It made her even more attractive.

More desirable.

Zageo decided he would pursue a relationship with her, regardless of whether it was an appropriate move for him or not. It had been a long time since he felt so vibrantly *alive* with a woman.

CHAPTER EIGHT

EMILY clasped her cheeks, willing the heat in them to recede. She'd splashed cold water on her face over and over again, but still it burned, her blood temperature at an all-time high from a chaotic mix of anger and fear.

She was furious with herself for succumbing to the stupid urge to discover what it might be like to be kissed by such a total foreigner, who just happened to be powerfully charged with sex appeal. Now he'd think she *was* a belly-dancing bedhopper. Besides which, it hadn't just been a kiss!

That man had to have the most wickedly exciting tongue in the world, not to mention knowing how to incite such a flood of passionate need, her breasts were still aching from it, her thighs felt like jelly, and the moist heat still lingering at their apex demonstrated an appalling carnal desire for a more intimate connection with him. She'd never felt like this with Brian!

And that thought made her feel even more uncomfortable. Disloyal. Brian had been her mate in every sense. She'd loved him. There'd never been anyone else. She'd never wanted anyone else. The sex they'd had together had seemed natural, good, answering their emotional needs at the time. It felt wrong to look back now and think it hadn't really been a potent force between them, not a nerve-shaking, mind-bending, stomach-twisting, overwhelmingly dominant force!

Though exploring these feelings further with a man who was forcibly holding her *under his protection* went totally against her grain. It was all very well for him to claim he was saving her from a nasty situation by not handing her over to local authorities. She still had no real freedom of movement. No free choices, either. And knowing herself innocent of any wrong-doing, she hated being a victim of circumstances.

It wasn't fair.

Being hugely attracted to a man who was so completely outside her possible relationship zone wasn't fair, either.

So what was she to do now?

Emily doused her face in cold water once again, wiped it dry, took several deep breaths, rolled her shoulders, then concentrated her mind on making a plan.

Until more checks into her background yielded the information which would be consistent with her account of herself, she might as well resign herself to being Zageo's *guest*, so why not pretend to be one? A guest would be sociable. A guest would show pleasurable anticipation in the exploration of the pristine coral reef around Pemba Island. More importantly, a guest's wishes should be taken into consideration and she could certainly challenge Zageo on that point.

Emily mentally girded her *guest* loins and set off to not only face the devil and the deep blue sea, but smile at both of them!

Amazingly, once she had accepted the idea of being taken on a delightful adventure, she really did enjoy herself. Fundu Lagoon looked like a great holiday retreat with its beach lodge and bungalows built from mangrove poles and palm thatch, giving the place a sense of fitting perfectly into the beautiful island environment, while still providing every modern convenience and equipment for all watersports.

The reefs around the island were fantastic; great, plunging walls of coral with all the colourful Indian Ocean marine life swimming and hunting in the wondrous playground. Distractions were plentiful, making Emily less conscious of how Zageo looked in a sleek black wetsuit and less sensitive about how she herself looked in the second-skin garment.

The sexual tension which she'd found so difficult to set aside while still on the boat, dissipated while they were underwater, sharing the pleasure of what they found and watched. It also helped that she had plenty to chat about after the dive, recalling what they'd seen, comparing it to experiences in other places.

They lunched at the beach lodge, sitting on a balcony overlooking the turquoise waters of the bay, hungrily demolishing servings of superb grilled fish, several different tasty salads and a platter of freshly sliced fruit.

Emily was thinking that now was the perfect time for a siesta when Zageo spoke, shattering any sense of safety her *guest* role had given her.

'We could retire to one of the bungalows.'

'What?' Her whole body jerked in shock at the suggestion which immediately conjured up images of sex in the afternoon.

'You looked sleepy,' he observed, watching her through his own lazily lowered lashes.

'Just feeling replete after such a lovely meal,' she quickly trotted out. 'Are we going to dive again this afternoon?'

'Do you want to?'

'I guess the question is…are you satisfied?'

He cocked one eyebrow as though considering which area of satisfaction she was referring to, and the sensual little curl of his lips was very suggestive of much more satisfaction being desired on many levels.

Emily's heart skipped a beat then rushed into beating so fast she suffered a dizzying rush of blood to the head. Words spilled into erratic speech. 'I meant your test. About me bëing a professional diver. You wanted to know if it was true. That's why we came here, wasn't it? For me to prove I wasn't lying?'

'It was one of the reasons.' The glimmer in his eyes suggested others were of more interest to him. 'I no longer have any doubt that you are comfortable with being underwater. But as to satisfaction…'

He *was* talking sex. She could hear it in the sensual purr of his voice, feel it in the prickling wash of it over her skin. Her stomach contracted with anxiety. It was difficult to fight her own ambivalent feelings. With Zageo feeding the tempting desire to simply give in and tangle intimately with him, she could barely remember why it would be stupid to do it.

Hannah…

Real life…

Shedding complications and getting directly to where she should be…

'Stone Town,' she said emphatically, cutting off whatever else Zageo might have put to her because all her instincts were quivering with the very real possibility of her becoming enmeshed in something she might never escape from. She pasted a brightly appealing smile on her face. 'Could we go to Stone Town now?'

He viewed her quizzically. 'You sister is not there, Emily.'

'You just spoke of satisfaction, Zageo,' she picked up pointedly. 'I've been aiming to get to Stone Town ever since I stepped foot on Jacques Arnault's yacht. That trip carried a load of unexpected stress and last night's swim and trek through the mangrove swamp wasn't a picnic, either. Now here I am, close to where I started out to be, and feeling really frustrated that you're holding me back from it.'

She heaved a feeling sigh and poured what she hoped was an eloquent plea into her eyes. 'If I could just have the satisfaction of going to The Salamander Inn myself…'

His mouth quirked into a sardonic smile. 'You don't believe me, Emily?'

'No more than you believe me, Zageo,' she shot back at him.

He shrugged, his dark eyes dancing with amusement. 'What reason would I have to lie?'

'I think you find me a novelty and since you have the power to play with me, that's what you're doing,' she stated unequivocally.

'A novelty…' He mused over the word, nodding as he spoke his thoughts. 'Something new…or is it something as old as time? Certainly you are not like other women I've known. Which I find intriguing. But *playing* with you…'

His eyes narrowed to glittering slits as though harnessing their penetrating power into intensely probing beams. Emily felt as though she was pinned inside his mental force-field and her heart was under attack. She couldn't think, couldn't move. She had to wait for him to release her from this eerily hypnotic connection.

'This is not a game, Emily,' he said quietly. 'It is a journey where the signposts are not clear, where the turnings are yet to be decided, where the destination is still obscure, yet…I will take it. And you will take it with me.'

Emily was swamped with a sense of inevitability. Her mind thumped with the certainty that whatever he willed was going to happen. She fought to assert her own individuality, to gain at least one foothold on the life she'd had before meeting *him*.

'Well, one signpost is very clear to me and that's Stone Town,' she insisted wildly. 'So why don't we go there right now before our journey takes us somewhere else?'

He laughed, tipping his head back in sheer uninhibited joy in the moment, making her pulse dance in a weird mixture of relief in the normality of laughter and a bubbling happiness at his pleasure in her.

'Are you sure you would not prefer to idle some time away in one of these bungalows first?' he teased, his eyes flirting with the promise of more physical pleasures. 'Indulge ourselves with some rest and relaxation under the cooling whirl of a fan…'

'With the air-conditioning in the saloon, we'll be cooler on the boat,' she quickly argued.

One black eyebrow arched wickedly. 'You do not wish to enjoy some heat?'

'It will still be hot in Zanzibar when we return there.'

'Why choose one satisfaction over another when you could have both?'

'It's as you said, Zageo. I don't have a clear signpost on anything but Stone Town.'

'Then we shall get Stone Town out of the way so we can progress beyond it.'

He rose purposefully to his feet and rounded the table to hold back her chair as she stood up, ready to leave. The zing of triumph at having won this concession from him was short-lived. He took firm possession of her hand for the walk through the beach lodge to the wharf which led back to the boat, and when she wriggled her fingers in a bid for freedom, his interlocked with hers, strengthening the hold.

Still a captive to his will, Emily thought, though he had ceded to her wishes on the destination issue. It was probably an indulgence he could well afford, letting her see the meeting place nominated by her sister. An unimportant sidetrack. The journey he wanted them to take revolved around physical contact and the insidiously distracting heat his hand generated was already beginning to erode her sense of purpose.

What was she going to achieve in Stone Town?

'How old were you when you met Brian, Emily?' Zageo asked as they reached the wharf and began the long stroll to the end of it where an outboard motorboat was waiting to transport them back to the cruiser.

Her mind gratefully seized on the reference to the man who had been the love of her life, hauling out the memory of their first meeting and blowing it up to blot out her current confusion. 'I was fourteen. His parents had just moved up to Cairns from the central coast of New South Wales and he came to my school that year.'

'School? How old was *he*?'

She smiled at the surprise in Zageo's voice. 'Sixteen. Tall and blond and very hunky. All the girls instantly developed crushes on him.'

'Did he play the field before choosing you?'

'No. Brian played it very cool, not linking up with anyone, just chatting around, but every so often I'd catch him watching me and I knew I was the one he liked.'

'The one he *wanted*,' came the sardonic correction.

Emily bridled at Zageo's personal slant on something he knew absolutely nothing about. 'It wasn't just the sex thing,' she flashed at him resentfully. 'Brian *liked* lots of things about me.'

'What's not to like?'

The slightly derisive retort was accompanied by a long sideways head to foot appraisal that shot Emily's temperature sky-high.

'I'm talking about the person I am inside,' she declared fiercely. 'Brian took the time to get to know me. He didn't take one look and decide what I was, as you've done!'

The accusation raised one mocking black eyebrow. 'On the contrary, despite what I'd call damning circumstances, I have continued to look at you, Emily, many times. And I am still gathering evidence as to your character.'

'But you don't care about it. You don't really care,' she hotly countered. 'You would have taken me to bed in one of those bungalows back there if I'd said yes.'

'You are not sixteen anymore, and sexual attraction does not wait upon niceties.'

'But I do have a choice over whether to give into it or not.'

The look he gave her ruthlessly blasted any hope she might be nursing about holding out on that score. Emily shrivelled inside herself, wishing she hadn't challenged him on it since they were on their way back to where a number of staterooms were readily available for intimate privacy. Not that he would stoop to raping her. He would disdain using force with a woman. But if he somehow trapped her into another kiss…

Extremely conscious of her vulnerability to his sexual magnetism, Emily kept her mouth firmly shut and her gaze averted from his as they rode in the outboard motorboat the island wharf to the air-conditioned cruiser. Zageo also remained silent but it was not a restful silence. The sense of purposeful power emanating from him had her nerves jangling and her mind skittering along wildly defensive lines.

At least he had agreed to take her to Stone Town.

Maybe Hannah would arrive any minute now.

Some action was needed to save her from this man and the sooner it came, the better.

CHAPTER NINE

ZAGEO maintained his darkly brooding silence until after they were served coffee in the saloon. Anxious to separate herself from any physical connection to the man who was now dominating her consciousness, Emily had seated herself in an armchair on one side of the low coffee table, but he sat opposite her, granting the relief of distance although there was no relief from the direct focus of his attention.

She listened to the powerful motors taking them back to Zanzibar, mentally urging them to make the trip as fast as possible. She was so wound up in willing the cruiser to speed them over the water, it came as a jolt when Zageo spoke.

'So…tell me the history of your relationship with the man you married,' he tersely invited.

The edge to his voice sounded suspiciously like jealousy, though Emily reasoned he simply didn't like coming off poorly in any comparison. Regardless of his motivation for seeking more knowledge of Brian, she

was only too eager to fill this dangerous time talking
about her one and only love, recalling shared experiences which had nothing to do with *sex*.

Words tumbled out, describing how from being school
sweethearts, she'd followed Brian into a career in the
tourist industry which was a huge part of the economy
in far north Queensland. They'd worked on dive boats,
been proficient in all water sports, crewed on cruise ships
that worked the coastline around the top end of Australia,
sailed yachts from one place to another for the convenience of owners to walk onto at any given time.

'When did you marry?' Zageo asked somewhat critically, as though the timing of the wedding had some
relevance to him.

'When I was twenty-one and Brian twenty-three.'

'A very young man,' he muttered deprecatingly.

'It was right for us!' she insisted.

'Marriage is about acquiring and sharing property,
having children. What do you have to show for the five
years you had together?'

'Marriage is also about commitment to each other.
We had a life of adventure…'

'And that's what you're left with? Adventure? Falling
into the company of a man like Jacques Arnault?' Zageo
remarked contemptuously. 'Your husband made no pro-
vision for your future, no—'

'He didn't know he was going to die!' she cut in, hating the criticism. 'The plan was to wait until we were
in our thirties before starting a family. After we'd been
everywhere we wanted to go.'

'Did it occur to you there is always another horizon?'

'What do you mean?'

He shrugged. 'Your Brian acted like a grown-up boy, still playing boys' games with the convenience of a committed companion. What if it was not in his psyche to ever settle down and provide a family home?'

'It's people who make a family, not a place,' she argued.

'You would have dragged your children around the world with him?'

'Why not? Experiencing the world is not a bad thing.'

'You have no attachment to your home country? Your home city?'

'Of course I do. It's always good to go back there. It's where my parents live. But Brian was my partner and wherever he went, I would have gone with him.'

Her vehemence on that point apparently gave Zageo pause for some reconsideration. His eyes narrowed and when he eventually made comment, it was laced with cynicism.

'Such devotion is remarkable. From my own experience of women in western society, I gathered that the old biblical attitude of—*whither thou goest, there goest I*—was no longer in play.'

'Then I'd say your experience was askew. I think it's still the natural thing for most women to go with the man they love. Certainly my sister did. When she married Malcolm, there was no question about her going to live with him on his farm in Zimbabwe. She just went.'

'Where exactly in Zimbabwe is this farm?'

'On what's called The High Veld,' Emily answered quickly, relieved to be moving onto a less sensitive subject. 'Malcolm is the third generation working this family owned land and although so much has changed in Zimbabwe he wants to hang onto it.'

Zageo shook his head. 'I doubt he will be able to. The process of reclaiming their country from foreign settlement is a priority with that government.'

Emily heaved a fretful sigh. 'Hannah is worried about the future. Especially for the children.'

'The two daughters.'

'Yes. Jenny is getting to school age and the local school has been closed down. Sally is only three.'

'Will both these young children be accompanying your sister to Zanzibar?'

Emily nodded. 'That was the plan.'

'How was this plan communicated to you?'

'Through a contact address I'd set up on the Internet.' The cloud of confusion that had made any clear path of action impossible suddenly lifted. 'That's what I have to do in Stone Town! Find an Internet Café!'

Zageo frowned at her. 'If you had told me this last night, Emily, there are Internet facilities at the palace. All you had to do—'

'I didn't think of it,' she cut in, throwing her hands out in helpless appeal. 'It was quite a shock being hauled into a place that conjured up thoughts of fairy-tale Arabian Nights, not to mention being confronted and cross-examined by a...a sheikh.'

A tide of heat rushed up her neck, telegraphing her acute embarrassment at being so fixated on him she couldn't even think sensibly, let alone logically. Horribly conscious of the scarlet flags burning in her cheeks, she swivelled in her chair to look out the saloon windows, ostensibly intent on watching their approach to Stone Town. The public harbour was coming into view and her whole body twitched with eagerness to get off the boat.

'Excuse me while I arrange for a car to meet us at the dock,' Zageo said.

'A car?' The pained protest burst from her lips and her gaze swung back to his, pleading for more freedom of movement. 'Couldn't we walk through the town to the inn? I've heard that the markets here are amazing. Besides, unless you know where an Internet café is…'

'There is no need to find a café. I offer you the Internet facilities at The Salamander Inn. We can go directly there so you can check for some communication from your sister.' He paused to underline the point before adding, 'Is it not your top priority?'

'Oh! Right! Thank you,' she rattled out, knowing she was cornered again and telling herself there was no point in fighting his arrangements.

Nevertheless, having to get into the black Mercedes which was waiting for them at the dock made her feel even more like a prisoner, trapped in an enclosed space with her captor and being forcibly taken to the place of his choice. Never mind that she did want to check out The Salamander Inn and she did want to get onto the Internet, doing both of them under Zageo's watchful eyes automatically held constraints she didn't like.

Common sense argued to simply accept being *his guest*—just sit back and enjoy being driven around in a luxury car. Except *he* was sitting beside her, dominating her every thought and feeling, making her intensely aware that he was sharing this journey and was intent on sharing a much longer and more intimate one with her. Apparently she had no choice about that, either.

Emily's nerves were so twitchy about the overwhelming nature of his current presence in her life, she evaded even glancing his way, staring fixedly out the tinted side-window, forcing her brain to register the images she saw in a desperate bid to wipe out the tormenting image of Sheikh Zageo bin Sultan Al Farrahn.

The problem was in its being far too attractive for any peace of mind; ridiculously attractive because he no more belonged in her world than she did in his; dangerously attractive because just the mental image of him was powerful enough to make her forget things she should be remembering.

'Pyramids,' she muttered, focusing fiercely on the market stalls lining both sides of the street on which they were travelling.

'I beg your pardon?'

She heaved a sigh at having broken a silence that probably should have been kept if she was to succeed in keeping Zageo at a distance. 'The stall keepers have stacked their fruit and vegetables into pyramids. I've never seen that before. I guess it must be some Egyptian influence. The people here seem to be such a melting pot of races,' she babbled, not looking at him, keeping her attention fastened *outside* the car. 'So far I've seen a Hindu temple, a mosque minaret and a Christian church spire, all in the space of a few hundred metres.'

'Egyptians, Phoenicians, Persians, Indians, even Chinese visited Zanzibar and settled here, along with the East Africans and traders from South Arabia,' Zageo informed her in a perfectly relaxed manner. 'Then, of course, the Portuguese took control of the island for two centuries. They've all left their influence on the native life and culture, including religion.'

Emily's mind seized on the Portuguese bit. She had thought Zageo looked Spanish but maybe his bloodline came from a neighbouring Latin country. 'Are you part Portuguese?' she asked, curiosity trapping her into looking directly at him.

He smiled, blitzing at least half her mind into registering that and nothing else, making her heart flip into a faster beat, causing her stomach to contract as though she had received a body-blow.

'My great-grandfather on my mother's side was Portuguese,' he finally replied, having done maximum damage with his smile. 'My great-grandmother was half-Indian, half-British. It makes for an interesting mix of races, does it not?'

'Your father is an Arab?' The half of her mind that was still working insisted that a sheikh couldn't get to be a sheikh without having a father who was pure Arab.

He nodded. 'Mostly. His grandmother was French. We are a very international family.'

'A very *wealthy* international family,' Emily said, deciding sheikhdom probably had more to do with who owned the oil wells.

He shrugged. 'Wealth that has benefited our people. And we keep investing to consolidate the wealth we have, ensuring that the future will have no backward steps. There is nothing wrong with wealth, Emily.'

'I didn't say there was. It just happens to form a huge gap between your circumstances and mine. And while you take all this for granted—' she waved wildly at their uniformed chauffeur and the plush interior of the Mercedes '—I hate not being able to pay my own way.' A passionate need for independence from him fired up other resentments. 'I hate not having my own money, my own credit card, my own…'

'Freedom to do whatever you want?'

'Yes!'

'Then why not feel free to be with me, Emily? It *is* what you want,' he claimed in that insidiously silky voice that slid straight under her skin and made all her nerve ends tingle.

His eyes mocked any attempt at denial. She struggled to come up with one that sounded sensible enough to refute his certainty. 'What we want is not always right for us, Zageo. Even you, with all the freedom your wealth gives you, must have been hit with that truth somewhere down the line.'

'Ah, but not at least to try it…to satisfy the wanting…how is one to make an informed judgment without embracing the experience?'

'I don't have to put my hand in a fire to know it will get burnt,' she slung at him and tore her gaze from the sizzling desire in his.

'You prefer to stay cold than hold out your hand to it, Emily? What of the warmth it promises? The sense of physical well-being, the pleasure…'

Her stomach contracted at the thought of the sexual pleasure he might give her. Panicked by how much she did want to try it, Emily seized the first distraction her gaze hit as the Mercedes started through a narrow alley.

'The doors…' Even on these poorer houses in the old part of Stone Town, they were elaborately carved and studded with very nasty looking iron or brass protrusions. 'Why are they made to look so intimidating?'

'The studs were designed to stop elephants from barging inside.'

'Elephants!' Emily was startled into looking incredulously at him. 'Are you telling me there are elephants rampaging around Zanzibar, even in the town?'

'No.' He grinned at having drawn her interest again. 'There have never been elephants on Zanzibar. The doors were originally made by Indian craftsmen who brought the design from their home country centuries ago. The style of them apparently appealed and has endured to the present day.'

She frowned, not liking them despite their elaborate craftsmanship. 'They give the sense of a heavily guarded fortress.'

'Very popular with tourists,' he drily informed her. 'They form one of Zanzibar's main exports.'

'What about spice? Isn't this island famous for its spice trade?'

'Unfortunately Zanzibar no longer has the monopoly on growing and selling cloves. Indonesia, Brazil, even China are now major producers. The island still has its plantations, of course, but they are not the economic force they once were.'

'That's rather sad, losing what made it unique,' Emily commented.

'The golden years of Zanzibar were not only based on the trade in cloves, but also in ivory and slaves, neither of which you would wish to revive,' he said, his eyes boring intently into hers. 'The past is the past, Emily. One has to move on.'

The words thudded into her heart—words she had recited to herself many times since being widowed. Zageo was making a pointedly personal message of them. But any journey with him would have to reach a dead end, forcing her *to move on* again. On the other hand, she certainly didn't regret her marriage. She might not regret a sexual dalliance with this sheikh, either.

She stared down at her hands which were tightly clasped in her lap, the fingers of her right hand automatically dragging at the ringless state of her left. What did she fear? The world famous model, Veronique, had taken Zageo as a lover. Why couldn't she? It wasn't a betrayal of her love for Brian. It was just something else. A different life experience.

Except she couldn't forget how out of control she'd been when he'd kissed her. To hand him that kind of power required an enormous amount of trust, and how could she give that trust to a man she hadn't even met before yesterday? To blithely act upon sheer attraction did not feel right, regardless of how strong the attraction was and no matter what Zageo argued.

She sucked in a deep breath, lifted her gaze and once more focused on the outside world. 'How much further is it to The Salamander Inn?' she asked, looking out at a veritable jumble of buildings, many of which were crumbling from sheer age.

'Not far. Perhaps another five minutes.'

'Why build an expensive hotel in this location?'

'It's the most historic part of Stone Town and tourists like local colour. They come to Zanzibar because of its exotic past and because its very name conjures up a romantic sense of the east, just like Mandalay and Kathmandu.' He smiled, his eyes wickedly teasing as he added, 'Sultans and slaves and spice…it's a potent combination.'

'For attracting the tourist dollar.'

'Yes,' he conceded, amused by her sidestep away from anything personal. 'And thereby boosting the economy of the island, generating more employment.'

'So this hotel is a benevolent enterprise on your part?' she half-mocked, wanting to get under *his* skin.

'I am, by nature, benevolent, Emily. Have I not kept you out of the local lock-up, giving you the benefit of the doubt, sympathising with your concern over your sister's whereabouts, offering you a free means of communication with her?' His eyes simmered with provocative promises as he purred, 'I wish you only what is good. And what will be good.'

It was futile trying to get the better of him. He was the kind of man who'd always be on top of any game he cared to play.

The car pulled up outside *his* hotel.

No doubt he could claim any suite he liked for his personal use.

Emily desperately tried telling herself she was only here to use a computer, but a wild sense of walking into the lion's den gripped her as Zageo escorted her into the foyer.

And came to a dead halt.

Right in front of them, impatiently directing a bell-boy on how to handle her luggage, was the stunningly beautiful and uniquely glamorous French-Moroccan model—Veronique!

CHAPTER TEN

EMILY could not help staring at the woman; the long glossy mane of black hair, flawless milk-coffee coloured skin, exotically tilted and thickly lashed chocolate-velvet eyes, a perfectly straight aristocratic nose, full pouty lips, and a cleanly sculptured chin that lifted haughtily at the sight of Zageo holding another woman's arm.

As well it might, Emily thought, suddenly feeling like a very common overcurvy peasant in her cotton skirt, casual little top, and very plain walking sandals. Apart from which, her own long hair was not exactly beautifully groomed after an underwater swim and her make-up was nonexistent.

Veronique's entire appearance was superbly put together. Her model-thin figure was wrapped in a fabulously elegant and sexy dark brown and cream polka-dot silk dress which screamed designer wear, and the high-heeled strappy sandals on her feet were so brilliantly stylish, anyone with a shoe fetish would have lusted for them. Her magnificent facial structure was highlighted with subtly toning make-up, her nails varnished a pearly cream, and just looking at the glossy black hair made Emily's feel like rats' tails.

'Veronique…this is a surprise,' Zageo said in his silky dangerous voice. Clearly it was not a surprise that pleased him.

'Your call last night felt like a call to arms, *cheri*,' she lilted, her tone warmly inviting him to take pleasure in her presence.

He'd called her last night?

Emily shot him a sharply inquiring look. Had he lied about having ended his relationship with Veronique?

'Then you were not listening to me,' he stated coldly.

Anger flashed from the supermodel's gorgeous dark eyes, flicked to Emily, then back to Zageo, having gathered a fierce determination to fight. 'You were mistaken in thinking I didn't want to be with you. I came to correct that misunderstanding.'

They were drawing attention from other people in the foyer. 'A private conversation should remain private,' Zageo cautioned sternly, signalling to the man behind the reception desk.

Instant action. A key was grabbed. The man ushered them to a door on the other side of the foyer. It opened to what was obviously the manager's domain, an office combined with a sitting area for conversations with guests.

Veronique stalked ahead, using the arrogant catwalk style of motion that automatically drew everyone's gaze after her. She was a star, intent on playing the star to the hilt, perhaps reminding Zageo of *who* she was, the kind of status she commanded.

'I can wait out here,' Emily suggested, pulling back from being witness to a lovers' quarrel and grasping what felt like the opportune moment to slip away entirely, extracting herself from a very sticky situation.

'*Oui,*' Veronique snapped over her shoulder.

'*Non!*' came Zageo's emphatic retort, forcibly steering Emily inside. 'Miss Ross is my guest and I will not do her the discourtesy of abandoning her for you, Veronique.'

It wasn't a discourtesy, Emily thought wildly, but again she was given no choice. *His* decision was punctuated by the door closing behind them.

Veronique wheeled to face them, jealous fury spitting from her eyes. 'You prefer *this woman* to me?'

On the surface of it, the preference seemed utter madness even to Emily's mind, so she didn't take offence, although a strong streak of female pride whispered that for a relationship to last—as her own with Brian had—there had to be more than surface stuff driving it. Two years, she reflected, was the usual timeframe for passion to wear thin.

Zageo ignored the question, blandly inquiring, 'How did you get from Paris to Zanzibar so quickly?'

The mane of hair was expertly tossed. 'You are not the only man I know who owns a private jet.'

If it was an attempt to make him jealous, it was a miserable failure, evoking only a curt, disdainful reply. '*Bien!* Then you'll have no problem with flying back tomorrow.'

Veronique scissored her hands in exasperated dismissal. 'This is absurd!'

'Yes, it is,' he agreed. 'I informed you of my position in no uncertain terms. Your coming will not change it.'

'But you misread my choice not to accompany you, Zageo.' She gestured an eloquent appeal. 'I wanted you to miss me. I wanted you to realise how good we are together. I wanted you to think about marrying me.'

'What?' Sharp incredulity in his voice. 'There was never any suggestion of a marriage being possible between us,' he thundered, hands lifting in such angry exasperation, Emily was able to slide out of his hold, quickly stepping over to the sofa against the wall, out of the firing line between the two antagonists.

'That doesn't mean it couldn't be,' Veronique argued.

'At no time did I lead you to think it. What we had was an arrangement, Veronique, an arrangement that suited both of us. You know it was so. Perhaps it does not suit you to have it ended, but I assure you, this attempt to push it further is futile.'

'Because of *her*?' A contemptuous wave and a venomous look were directed at Emily.

It was a good question, Emily thought, curious to know the answer herself since the ruction between Veronique and the sheikh had only occurred last night. She tore her gaze from the glittering double fangs of Veronique's eyes to look at Zageo, and was instantly shafted by two laser beams burning into her brain.

'Because its time was over,' he answered, speaking directly to Emily, his eyes hotly impressing the point.

'I had decided that before Miss Ross walked into my life.'

Curiously enough, it was a relief to hear this. Being the source of breaking up a long-standing relationship would not have sat easily with her, although she had done absolutely nothing to effect such an outcome.

'But you've let her sweeten the decision, haven't you?' came the furious accusation. '*She* is why you won't take me back. So what has *she* got that I have not, Zageo? What does *she* give you that I did not?'

Emily's cheeks burned.

Nothing, she thought, hating being dragged into what was definitely not her business.

But Zageo was still looking at her and the heat in his eyes simmered with needs and desires that were focused on her, making her heart catapult around her chest, flipping her stomach, shooting her mind into chaos as it tried to deal with responses that were scattering her wits.

'How does one compare a hothouse carnation to a wild water-lily?' he rolled out in a softer tone that somehow caused goose-bumps to erupt all over Emily's skin. 'It is foolish to try to measure the differences. Each has its own unique appeal.'

A wild water-lily?

Emily wasn't used to hearing such flowery language from a man, though her heart was thumping its own wanton appreciation of it even as she tried to force her mind into reasoning that this was definitely Arabian Nights stuff, totally surreal, and she *must not* let herself get caught up in it.

Zageo's riveting gaze finally released hers, turning back to the woman who had so recently been his intimate companion. 'Please…do not lower yourself with these indignities,' he urged, appealing for a cessation of personal hostilities. 'Our time together is over. Yesterday is yesterday, Veronique. Tomorrow is tomorrow.'

'You see how it is?' she shot at Emily, highly incensed by the comparison she had forced by her own angry diatribe. 'No doubt you have been as swept away by him as I was. But it will only last for as long as the arrangement suits his convenience. He might not look like an Arab but he is one at heart.'

'An Arab whose generosity is being severely tested.' The warning was delivered with a hard look of ruthless intent. 'Do you want to continue this spiteful scene or do you want the Paris apartment?'

Veronique delivered another expert toss of her hair as she disdainfully returned her attention to him. 'I was doing Miss Ross a kindness, Zageo, informing her of the bottom line so she's not completely blinded by your beauty.'

'You are intent on poisoning something you do not understand,' he whipped at her. 'Make your decision now, Veronique.'

The threat whirling in the air forced the supermodel to take stock. She was not winning. And regardless of her star status, Sheikh Zageo bin Sultan Al Farrahn was by far the more influential person here in Zanzibar, with the power to make her visit very unpleasant. The bottom line was she hadn't been welcomed and had worn out his patience with making herself even less welcome.

She inhaled a deep breath, calming herself, pulling a mask of pride over her more volatile emotions. 'I could not bring myself to believe what you said last night,' she offered in a more considered appeal. 'I came to mend fences.'

It made no difference. He simply replied, 'I'm sorry you put yourself to that trouble.'

She tried a rueful sigh. Her hands fluttered an apologetic appeal. 'Okay, I took our relationship for granted. I won't do it again.'

He gave no sign of softening, implacably stating, 'If you had truly valued it, you would have made different decisions.'

'I do have modelling assignments lined up throughout the next three months,' she quickly excused.

'I offered you my private jet to get to them.'

He was giving her no room to manoeuvre, not so much as a millimetre. Veronique had no choice but to accept their affair was over. Emily felt a stab of sympathy for her, having been subjected to no choice herself at this man's hands.

'I will take the apartment, *cheri*,' came the final decision, bitter irony lacing her voice as she added, 'I've grown fond of it.'

He nodded. 'Consider it settled. I shall inform the manager here that you are my guest at the inn until you return to Paris. Tomorrow?'

'*Oui.* Tomorrow I shall put all this behind me.'

'*Bien!*' Zageo strode to the desk, proceeding to call the manager on the in-house telephone system.

Veronique subjected Emily to a glare that seethed

with malevolence, belying the resigned acceptance of the kiss-off apartment and suggesting that if the model could do her supposed replacement an injury on the sly, she would not hesitate to uproot the wild water-lily and take huge satisfaction in tearing it to pieces.

Emily was glad the supermodel would be flying away from Zanzibar tomorrow. She had enough trouble on her hands without having to deal with the fury of a scorned woman. Besides, the fault behind this situation did not lie at her door. Zageo had made that very clear. On the other hand, it would have been much clearer if he hadn't made the break-up call last night.

The manager of the inn knocked and entered the tension-packed room, warily closing the door behind him as he awaited more instructions from the sheikh. Zageo waved to the computer on the desk, requesting the password for Internet access to be written down for his use. This jolted Emily into remembering the purpose which had brought them here. It amazed her that Zageo had not been distracted from it. She certainly had.

The manager quickly complied. He was then asked to escort Veronique to a guest suite and ensure her needs were met. The main current of tension in the room swept out with the supermodel's exit, leaving Emily feeling like a very limp water-lily, trapped into waiting for the strong flow that would inevitably come from Zageo.

He beckoned her to the desk where he was already tapping away on the computer keyboard. Emily took a deep breath and pushed her feet forward, trying desperately to put the thought of contact with her sister in a more important slot than contact with Zageo. Hannah was her reason for being here. She could not let a totally unsuitable attraction to this man cloud that issue.

She took the chair he invited her to take in front of the computer. Her fingers automatically performed the functions necessary to access her e-mail. The tightness in her chest eased slightly as Zageo moved away, choosing not to intrude on her private correspondence.

Whether this meant he did finally believe her story or whether it was simply ingrained courtesy on his part, Emily didn't know and didn't let it concern her. A message from Hannah was on the screen. It was dated the same day Emily had woken up from a drugged sleep on Jacques's yacht to find he didn't have a wife onboard and she was the only member of his crew and they were already at sea.

Emily—I hope this reaches you before you set sail for Zanzibar. I won't make it there. Can't. We didn't get very far before running into an army patrol and it didn't matter what I pleaded, the men confiscated everything and called Malcolm to come and get me and the girls. We're all under house arrest now. Not allowed to leave the farm to go anywhere. I'm half expecting the phone lines to be cut, as well, so if you don't receive another message from me, they will have stopped all outside communication.

I'm scared, Emily. I've never been so scared. I don't mind standing by Malcolm but I wish I'd managed to get the girls out. You could have taken them home

to Mum and Dad in Australia. There is so much un-
rest in this country and I just don't know if these
troubles will pass or get worse.
Anyhow, I'm sorry we won't be meeting up. And
please don't think you can come here and do something because you can't. So stay away. It won't help.
Understand? I'll let you know what's happening if I
can. Lots of love, Emily. I couldn't have had a better
little sister. Bye for now. Hannah.

Emily didn't realise she'd stopped breathing as she
took in the words on the screen. Shock and fear chased
around her mind. This was the last message from her sister. The last one. It was a week old. Seven days of silence.

'Emily? Is something wrong?'

She looked up to find Zageo watching her, his brow
lowered in concern. The trapped air in her lungs
whooshed out as she mentally grappled with Hannah's
situation. Her mouth was too dry to speak. She had to
work some moisture into it.

'Hannah is a prisoner in her own home,' she finally
managed to blurt out, silently but savagely mocking
herself for railing against being Zageo's prisoner. That
was a joke compared to what her sister was going
through—her sister and nieces and brother-in-law.

'They might be dead now, for all I know,' she muttered despairingly.

'Dead?'

'Read it for yourself!' she hurled at him as she

erupted from the chair, driven by a frantic energy to pace around the room, to find some action that might help Hannah. 'You wanted proof of my story?' Her arm swept out in a derisive dismissal of his disbelief. 'There it is on the screen!'

He moved over to the desk, accepting the invitation to inform himself.

Emily kept pacing, her mind travelling in wild circles around the pivotal point of somehow getting Hannah and her family to safety, right out of Zimbabwe if possible. She did not have the power or the resources to achieve such an outcome herself, but what of the Australian Embassy? Would someone there help or would diplomatic channels choke any direct action?

She needed someone strong who could act…would act…

'This is not good news,' Zageo muttered.

Understatement of the year, Emily thought caustically, but the comment drew her attention to the man who arranged his world precisely how he wanted it, wielding power over her without regard to any authority but his own. She stopped pacing and gave him a long hard look, seeing what had previously been a very negative aspect of him as something that could become a marvellous positive!

Maybe…just maybe…Sheikh Zageo bin Sultan Al Farrahn could achieve what she couldn't.

Veronique had said he owned a private jet. Almost certainly a helicopter, too, Emily reasoned. With pilots on standby to fly them.

Building his hotel chain throughout Africa must have given him powerful political contacts in the countries where he'd invested big money. Apart from which, his enormous wealth could probably bribe a way to anywhere. And out of anywhere.

Zageo wanted her in bed with him.

Emily had no doubt about that.

He'd also once wanted Veronique in bed with him—and for the satisfaction of that desire he'd been prepared to give away what was surely a multimillion dollar apartment in Paris.

A hysterical little laugh bubbled across Emily's brain. Jacques had tried to trade her to the sheikh in return for his freedom, and here she was, planning to trade herself to him for her sister's freedom.

Which would turn her into the whore he'd first thought her.

Emily decided she didn't care.

She'd do anything to secure the safety of Hannah and her family.

She'd try the trade.

CHAPTER ELEVEN

ZAGEO parted from Emily as soon as they returned to the palace. He wanted to alleviate her distress, if possible, by finding out if the Coleman family had survived this past week. He had instructed Abdul to pursue inquiries in Zimbabwe, so some useful information might have already been acquired.

Zageo no longer had any doubt that Emily had spoken the truth all along, and everything he'd learnt about her made her a more fascinating and desirable woman, certainly not one he'd want to dismiss from his life at this early juncture.

They would meet for dinner, he'd told her, hoping to give her news that would clear the worry from her eyes. He wanted her to see that having his favour was good. He wanted her to look at him with the same deep and compulsive desire he felt for her. And he wanted her to give into it.

Abdul was in his office, as usual, more at home with his communications centre than anywhere else. He was amazingly efficient at keeping track of all Zageo's business and personal interests. If he didn't have the information required at his fingertips, it was relentlessly pursued until it was acquired.

'The Coleman family…' Zageo prompted once the appropriate courtesies had been exchanged.

Abdul leaned back in the chair behind his desk, steepling his hands over his chest in a prayerful manner, indicating that he'd decided this issue was very much in the diplomatic arena. 'The M written in the register at The Salamander Inn stands for Malcolm. His wife's name is Hannah. They have two young daughters—'

'Yes, yes, I know this,' Zageo cut in, quickly recounting the e-mail he'd read at the inn to bring Abdul up-to-date on where the situation stood to his knowledge. 'The critical question is…are they still alive?'

'As of today, yes,' Abdul answered, much to Zageo's relief.

He could not have expected Emily to be receptive to him if she was in a state of grief over the deaths of people he had never met. She would want to go home to her parents in Australia, and in all decency, he would have had to let her go.

'However…' Abdul went on ominously, 'I would call their position perilous. Malcolm Coleman has been too active in protesting the policies of the current regime. His name is on a list of public antagonists who should be silenced.'

'Is the danger immediate?'

'If you are concerned for their safety, I think there is time to manoeuvre, should you wish to do so.'

'I wish it,' Zageo answered emphatically.

There was a long pause while Abdul interpreted his sheikh's reply. 'Do I understand that Miss Ross will be staying with us beyond Monday, Your Excellency?'

'Given that her sister's family can be rescued, yes, I have decided Miss Ross's companionship will add immeasurably to my pleasure in this trip around our African properties.'

'Ah!' Abdul nodded a few times and heaved a sigh before bringing himself to address the problem posed by Emily's family. 'Quick action will be needed. The pressure is on for Malcolm Coleman to give up his farm and leave the country but he is persisting in resisting it. Defying it.'

'Intent on fighting for what he considers his,' Zageo interpreted.

Abdul spread his hands in an equitable gesture. 'It is a large and very profitable farm that has been in his family for three generations. It is only natural for a man to wish to hold onto his home.'

'There will be no home with himself and his family dead,' Zageo commented grimly. 'He must be persuaded to accept that reality.'

'Precisely. Even so, to walk away with no recompense…'

'See if we can buy his farm. It will allow him to leave with his pride intact, giving him the financial stake he might need to start over in another country and still be successful in the eyes of his wife and children.'

'You want to acquire property in Zimbabwe?' Abdul queried somewhat incredulously.

'Very briefly. Perhaps it can be used as barter for the Colemans's safe passage out of the country. Find a recipient in the regime who understands favours, Abdul. The idea of acquiring a profitable farm without paying a cent might appeal. Delivery on delivery.'

'Ah! A diplomatic resolution.'

'Behind doors.'

'Of course, Your Excellency.'

Zageo relaxed, reasonably confident that his plan could be effected. Tonight he would tell Emily that not only was her sister's family still amongst the living, he had also set in motion the steps to extract them from their dangerous situation.

She would want to stay with him then.

She would want to know firsthand the outcome of his rescue plan.

It might not be bending to his will but…Zageo decided that winning her favour was the best way to gaining her submission. In fact, it would give him much satisfaction to arrange a meeting between Emily and her sister. This could not be held in Stone Town. He had to move on. Nevertheless, he would give Emily Ross what she had come for.

Delivery…for delivery.

CHAPTER TWELVE

BACK in the women's quarters of the palace, Emily
wasted no time in organizing what she wanted done.
Zageo had said they would meet for dinner. With the
image of Veronique still vividly in her mind, the presen-
tation of herself with the view of becoming his mistress
definitely required perfect grooming, artful make-up
and sexy clothes. Since her own luggage contained
nothing that could be described as seductively tempting…

'The trunk of belly-dancing costumes…do you still
have it, Heba?'

'Yes. Will I have it brought to you?' she offered
obligingly.

Emily nodded. 'Let's see if we can find something
really erotic in it.'

That was certainly what Zageo had expected of her
last night so let him have it tonight, Emily reasoned, deciding that an in-your-face statement of her intention
was more telling than a thousand words.

She chose a hot-pink costume with beaded bands in black and silver. The bra was designed to show optimum cleavage. The skirt was slinky, clinging to hips, bottom and upper thighs where it was slit for freedom of leg movement. The edges of the slits were beaded as well, making them very eye-catching.

'It is a bold costume,' Heba commented somewhat critically.

'I have to be bold tonight,' Emily muttered, beyond caring what the women who were attending to her needs thought.

Only one thing was important.

Getting the sheikh *to do something* about Hannah and her family.

She had her mind steeled to deliver her part of the trade, yet when the summons to dinner came, a nervous quivering attacked her entire body. What she was setting out to do wasn't *her*. Yet she had to pull it off. If something terrible happened to Hannah and she hadn't done anything to help, she would never forgive herself.

Besides, it wasn't as though she was unattracted to Zageo. It could well be a fantastic experience, having sex with him. She couldn't imagine he'd want a long relationship with her. The stunningly beautiful and glamorous Veronique, who shared his jet set class, had only held his interest for two years. Emily figured on only being a brief novelty, possibly lasting for the duration of his tour of the Al Farrahn hotels. Once he returned to his normal social life, she'd be a fish out of water—one he would undoubtedly release.

So, what were a few months out of her own life compared to the lives of Hannah and her family? She had no commitments. There was nothing to stop her from offering herself as a bed companion to a man who might or might not take up some time which was of no particular use to her anyway.

The costume trunk had also yielded a black silk cloak which Emily employed to cover herself while being escorted to the sheikh's private apartment. She was ushered into the same opulent sitting room where Zageo had commanded her presence last night. He was back in his sheikh clothes, the long white tunic and richly embroidered over-robe in purple and gold, making her feel even more nervous about his foreignness.

However, she was not about to baulk at doing what she had to do. The moment the door closed behind the men on escort duty, she whipped off the cloak, determined on getting straight to business. However, instead of exciting speculative interest in Zageo, her appearance in the provocative belly-dancing costume evoked an angry frown.

'What is this?' he demanded, the harsh tone making her heart skitter in apprehension. His eyes locked onto hers with piercing intensity. 'You claimed the costumes did not belong to you.'

'They don't! I just thought…' She swallowed hard, fighting to prevent her throat from seizing up. 'I thought it would please you to see me dressed like this.'

'Please me…' He spoke the words as though this was a strange concept to be examined for what it meant. His gaze narrowed, then skated down over the bared curves of her body, seemingly suspicious of their sexual promise.

Emily's heart was thundering in her ears, making it difficult to think over its chaotic drumming. She told herself she should be moving forward, swaying her hips like a belly-dancer, showing herself willing to invite him to touch, to kiss, to take whatever gave him pleasure. A sexy woman would slide her arms around his neck, press her body to his, use her eyes flirtatiously. It was stupid, stupid, stupid to stand rooted to the spot, barely able to breathe let alone shift her feet.

'Why would you suddenly set out to please me, Emily?'

She trembled. His voice was laced with *dis*pleasure. She was hit with such deep confusion she didn't know what to do or say. Her hands lifted in helpless appeal, needing to reach out to him yet frightened now of being rebuffed, spurned, sent away.

'For the past twenty-four hours you have been determined on putting distance between us,' he mockingly reminded her.

The heat of shame scorched her cheeks. What she planned was the act of a whore. There was no denying it. The trade was too blatant. She hadn't thought it would matter to him as long as she gave him the satisfaction of having what he wanted. But as he strolled towards her, the sardonic little smile curling his mouth made her feel she had lost whatever respect she had won with him.

'Now what could have inspired this change of attitude?' he queried, his brilliant dark eyes deriding any attempt at evasion. 'Was it the proof that my relationship with Veronique is over?'

'That…that does help,' she choked out, realising that the break-up arrangement had contributed a great deal to her thinking. Though it didn't excuse it. No, it was desperation driving this deal and Emily was suddenly afraid Zageo would find that offensive.

He moved around behind her, lifting her long hair back over her shoulder to purr in her ear, 'So…you are now ready to take this journey with me. You *want* to take it. You *want* to feel my touch on your skin.' He ran soft fingertips down the curve of her spine. 'You *want* me to taste all of you.' He trailed his mouth down her throat, pressing hot sensual kisses. 'Let me hear you say that, Emily.'

Her hands had fallen to her sides. They were clenching and unclenching as waves of tension rolled through her. She sucked in a quick breath and started pushing out the necessary words. 'You can do…you can do… whatever you like with me—'

'No, no, that sounds far too passive,' he cut in before she could complete spelling out the deal. 'Though now that you have given me permission…'

He unclipped the bra and slid the straps off her shoulders. As the beaded garment started to fall from her breasts, the sheer shock of being so swiftly bared, jolted Emily into defensive action. Her hands whipped up, catching the cups and plastering them back into place.

'Did you mean to tease me, Emily? Have I spoilt your game?' he asked in the silky dangerous tone that shot fearful quivers through her heart. Even as he spoke, his hands glided up from around her waist and covered her own, his fingers extending further than the bra cups to fan the upper swell of her breasts. 'No matter,' he assured her. 'I'm on fire for you anyway.'

'Stop,' she finally found voice enough to gasp out. 'Please…stop.'

'This does not please you?'

'No…yes…no…I mean…'

'What do you mean, Emily?'

His voice was now like a sharp-edged knife, slicing into her. Tears of confusion welled into her eyes. This scene was going—had gone—all wrong. She simply wasn't sophisticated enough to bring off the subtle sexual bartering that went on in his world.

'I'll take this journey with you if you'll help my sister,' she blurted out in wild desperation.

'And you will withhold yourself if I do not agree? You will push me away, refasten your bra, and scorn my desire for you?' The whiplike edge to his voice gathered more intensity as he added, 'Not to mention your desire for me.'

It sounded horrible. Everything decent in Emily recoiled from using sex as a bargaining tool. It eliminated any good feelings that might have eventuated from being intimate with this man. She shook her head in hopeless shame and humiliation.

'I'm sorry…sorry…I didn't know what else to do.'

'Little fool,' he growled. 'Playing a game that is not in your nature.'

His hands dropped to her waist and spun her around

to face him. He cupped her face, his fingers gently sweeping the trickle of tears from her cheeks. The tender gesture was in perverse contrast to the glittering anger in his eyes.

'Did you imagine I was not aware of your distress over your sister and her family?'

'They are nothing to you,' she choked out in a ragged plea for his understanding.

'*You* are not nothing to me, Emily.'

'I was counting on that,' she confessed.

'Yet you did not credit me with caring enough to do whatever I could to ease your distress?'

His words seethed with deep offence. Emily frantically seized on what she thought were mitigating circumstances. 'I don't know you,' she pleaded. 'All I know is you've kept me here to…to play with me.'

'Play with you,' he repeated in a scoffing tone that stirred Emily's blood, triggering a flood of volatile feelings that instantly threatened to burst out of control.

She wrenched her head out of his hold, stepping back to let fly at him with her own tirade of deep offence. 'You've had me jumping through hoops ever since I was forced into your company. First, you play the grand inquisitor, deliberately choosing not to believe a word I said. After which, you left me no alternative but to dress up as a belly-dancer for you…'

'Which you have no problem doing tonight,' he sliced at her.

'Because you made it your game, Zageo,' she asserted vehemently. 'I was only trying to fit into it.'

'Fine! Then fit!'

Before Emily could even draw breath to utter another word, he swooped on her, swept her off her feet, and in a dizzying whirl of movement, carried her through the sitting room and beyond it to another lamp-lit room where he tipped her onto a pile of exotic silk and satin cushions spread across a massive, four-poster bed. Her arms flew out to stop herself from rolling. The bra became dislodged again and Zageo whipped it off, leaving her naked from head to hips.

'No backtracking now, Emily,' he fired at her. 'We have a deal. In return for my services in rescuing your family, you've agreed to let me do whatever I like with you. Right?'

The violence of his feelings made her pulse beat faster, increasing the wild agitation racing through her. 'How do I know you'll help?' she cried, alarmed by the thought he would just do what he wanted anyway.

'Because I am a man of honour who always delivers on a deal,' he stated savagely.

He was shedding his robe, hurling it away. She scrambled to sit up, acutely aware of her full breasts swinging as she did so and realising her nipples had tightened in some instinctive response to the raking heat in his eyes.

'Are you a woman of your word, Emily?' he challenged, discarding his tunic and underpants with swift and arrogant carelessness while fiercely warning her, 'Leave that bed and you leave with nothing from me.'

She sat utterly still, staring at him, not because of the

threat but because he looked so stunningly magnificent. She had seen many almost naked men, especially guys who excelled in water sports, and they invariably had well-honed physiques—broad shoulders, flat stomachs, lean hips, powerfully muscled thighs. Zageo had all that but somehow his body was far more pleasingly proportioned.

It emanated an aura of indomitable male strength without the overdelineated musculature that came from excessive weight lifting at a gym. And his dark olive skin gleamed with a taut smoothness that incited an almost compelling desire to touch. Emily was not an expert on judging men's sexual equipment, but the sight of Zageo's certainly set up flutters of nervous excitement.

He stepped forward, his hands virtually spanning her waist as he lifted her into standing on the bed. 'Unfasten the skirt,' he commanded. 'Show me how willing you are to do whatever I want.'

Impossible to back down now, she told herself. The challenge blazing from his eyes seared her own sense of honour, forcing her past the point of no return. He'd taken the deal. She had to deliver.

As she reached around to the zipper at the pit of her back, he released her waist and lifted his hands to her naked breasts, rotating his palms over the taut peaks, making them acutely sensitive to his touch, driving arcs of piercing pleasure from her nipples to below her belly and causing Emily to gasp at the intensity of the feeling.

The unfastened skirt slithered down to pool around her feet. Her gasp turned to a moan of yearning as the almost torturous caress of her breasts ceased. Her hands curled urgently around Zageo's shoulders, unconsciously kneading them in a blind desire for continuity. He bent his head, his mouth swiftly ministering the sweetest balm to her need, licking and sucking as he hooked his thumbs into her panties and drew this last piece of clothing down her legs.

She stepped out of the restricting garment without a moment's hesitation, her previous inhibitions erased by the excitement coursing through her. He stroked her inner thighs, making them quiver, making her stomach contract in wild anticipation as he moved a hand into the slickened folds of her sex, fingers sliding over the moist heat that had been building and building from the erotic ministration of his mouth on her breasts.

Every one of her internal muscles tensed, waiting for a more intimately knowing touch, wanting it, craving it. Slowly his fingers slid inside, moving as deeply as they could, undoubtedly feeling the pulsing welcome her body gave instinctively. They withdrew to circle the entrance tantalisingly while his thumb found and caressed her clitoris, increasing an erotic pressure on it as his fingers pushed in again. And again. And again.

Emily's whole body bent like a bow, driven to an exquisite tension, blinding pleasure consuming every cell and needing to burst into some further place, reaching for it...reaching...the momentum escalating, then breaking past a barrier that was almost pain to shatter .

into a flood of melting sweetness, her knees buckling at the intensity of the waves sweeping through her.

Zageo caught her as her hands lost their purchase on his shoulders, carrying her with him as he plunged onto the bed, lying her flat on her back amongst the cushions and hovering over her, his eyes glittering fierce satisfaction in her helpless response to him.

He lifted her arms above her head, pinning them there with his own. They were simply too limp to resist the action though she knew intuitively this was a deliberate expression of domination over her and at another time and place she would have fought it. He clearly exulted in what he saw as submission to his will.

Emily smiled. Right here and now she didn't care what he thought. Her body was humming its own exultation. His gaze fastened on her smile. His mouth quirked into a cruel little twist and swooped on it, his lips hard and hungry, forcing hers apart, his tongue driving deep, intent on stirring another storm of sensation. *Her* blissful contentment was irrelevant. This was all about him taking his pleasure and he was the one who had to feel satisfied.

Some primitive streak inside her insisted on contesting the ruthless ravishment of his kiss. Her tongue duelled with his, sparking a passionate fight for possession. He might have the use of her body for a while but she hadn't traded any of her spirit. If he'd imagined getting a tame sex-slave, he could think again.

So consumed was Emily with the need to hold her own in this kiss, when Zageo released her arms she grabbed his head, instinctively moving to wrest back some control over what was happening. She was so caught up in trying to match his wildly erotic plunder, the lifting of her lower body took her by surprise. The shock of him entering her caused a total lack of focus on anything other than the sensation of his hard flesh moving past the soft convulsions of her own, tunnelling to her innermost depths, filling what had remained empty for a long, long time.

The jolt of that intensely satisfying fullness took Emily straight to the edge of climax again. Everything within her pulsed to the rhythmic beat of his smooth and powerful thrusts—each withdrawal setting up a drum-roll of exquisite anticipation, each plunge sending her hurtling into a tumultuous sea of ecstasy.

She heard herself moaning, crying out—totally involuntary sounds issuing from her throat. She was barely conscious of her hands squeezing his buttocks, instinctively goading, wanting the rocking to be harder, faster, wilder, until the waves turned into one continuously rolling crest, the explosive spasms of his climax driving it, and she floated off into a space where she was only anchored by him, his arms wound securely around her as she lay on his chest—a heaving chest that felt like the gentle swell of calmer waters after riding through a tempest.

Emily didn't move, didn't attempt to say anything. Not only was she in a daze of sensory overload, she had no idea what should or would come next. Besides, her whole experience of this man was that he took the lead in any activity to be shared with him. Moreover, the bargain she'd made put him in charge of her life. There was no point in even stirring until he showed some desire for it.

He stroked her back, making her skin tingle with pleasure. He certainly knew how to touch a woman, Emily thought, silently marvelling at the incredibly fantastic sexual experience he had just given her. If this was a sample of what she'd have to *endure* at his hands to keep her side of the trade, it was absolutely no hardship.

In fact, she understood why Veronique had come flying to Zanzibar to get him back. It was not going to be easy to say goodbye and walk away from what he gave. Not even an apartment in Paris would make up for having lost a lover of his calibre. Emily had a sneaking suspicion that the memory of what Zageo had just done to her would be a pinnacle of pleasure she might never reach with anyone else. Not even with Brian...

She clamped down on that thought. It was wrong to make comparisons. This relationship—if it could be called that—was something very different to her marriage. It was a slice of life she hadn't been looking for, eventuating from circumstances over which she'd had no control.

Anxiety welled up as she thought of Hannah, fraying the langour she had succumbed to in Zageo's soothing embrace. He was playing with her hair, lifting up the long tresses and letting them trail around his fingers, and as though he sensed her change of mood, he suddenly bunched her hair in his hand, slightly tugging to grab her attention.

'They are alive,' he said.

'What?' His statement seemed surreal, as though he had just read her mind.

'Your sister, her husband and daughters…they are alive. Do not be imagining them dead because it is not so,' he gruffly declared.

Adrenaline shot through Emily's sluggish veins. She bolted up to scan his eyes for truth, breaking his embrace and planting her own arms on either side of his head to lean over him in his current supine position. 'How do you know?' she demanded.

One black eyebrow arched in mocking challenge. 'You question my knowledge?'

She huffed with impatience. 'Not your knowledge, Zageo. I'm asking how you came by it.'

'Given that your sister had not arrived at the inn, as you had expected, I left instructions that her whereabouts be traced while we were out today,' he answered matter-of-factly. 'When we returned from Stone Town…'

'Are they under house arrest as Hannah feared?' Emily pressed, filled with an urgency to know what problems her sister was facing.

'Yes. But the point I am making, my dear Emily, is—' he ran a finger over her lips to silence any further intemperate outburst '—they are alive. And I shall now take every step I can to guarantee their future safety.'

Relief poured through her. Trading herself for this outcome had been worthwhile. No matter how big a sacrifice of her own self it might become, she would not regret making it. Some positive action would be taken to help Hannah.

'What do you plan to do?' she queried eagerly.

'Enough!' He surged up, catching her off-guard and rolling her onto her back, swiftly reestablishing his domination. The fingers that had been teasing her lips now stroked her jawline as though testing it for defiance. His dark eyes gleamed with a ruthless desire to re-acquaint her with the trade she'd made. 'You will trust me to negotiate your sister's freedom as best I can. How I do it is not your business. It is your business to please me, is it not?'

Had she?

Doubts whirled, attacking her natural self-confidence.

Was he satisfied with what he'd had of her so far?

Before tonight her sexual experience had been limited to one man—a man who'd had no other woman but herself. Her heart stampeded into thumping with panic as she thought of the high-living, sophisticated Veronique. She didn't know how to compete.

'You'll have to tell me what you want me to do,' she pleaded, frightened of being inadequate.

'Oh, I will,' he promised, smiling some deeply sensual and private satisfaction.

And he did.

Emily didn't mind doing any of it.

The happy knowledge that Hannah and her family were alive bubbled at the back of her mind, but in the forefront of it was the amazing truth that being intimately entangled with Sheikh Zageo bin Sultan Al Farrahn was making her feel more vibrantly alive than *she* had ever felt in her life.

CHAPTER THIRTEEN

ON MONDAY they flew to Kenya.

'But it's in the opposite direction to Zimbabwe,' Emily had protested.

An instant flash of anger had answered her. 'Do you doubt that I will deliver on my promise?'

'It just doesn't seem logical to travel there,' she had temporised warily. 'If you'd explain…'

'The negotiations to secure the safety of your sister's family will take time. We must move through diplomatic channels. While this is proceeding, there is little point in my not keeping to my own schedule. And you will accompany me—' his eyes had stabbed a challenge to her commitment '—as agreed.'

Again there was no choice but to go his way.

And as usual, it turned out that *his* way gave Emily an immense amount of amazing pleasure and it wasn't all exclusively connected to the intense sexual passion he could and did repeatedly stir.

The hotel he was checking on in Kenya was unlike

any hotel she had ever seen. It was, in fact, a safari resort, and the rooms were designed to look like a series of mud huts nestled cunningly around a hillside overlooking the Serengetti Plain. Inside they provided every luxury a traveller might want while the decor made fascinating use of the brightly colourful beading and fabrics much loved by the Masai tribe.

Best of all was the magnificent vista from every window—great herds of wildebeest grazing their way across the vast rolling plain which was dotted here and there by the highly distinctive acacia trees with their wide flat tops. It was also a surprising delight to see so many species of wild animals just roaming free, totally ignoring the intrusion by mankind.

When she and Zageo were taken out in one of the special safari vans, they might have been in an invisible spaceship for all the notice the animals took of them. A pride of lions, resting in the long grass by one of the tracks, didn't even turn their heads to look at the vehicle. In another place, a cheetah was teaching her three young cubs to hunt with absolutely no distraction from her mission, despite a number of vans circling to give their passengers a view of the action. Real life in Africa, Emily kept thinking, feeling very privileged to see it firsthand.

It had far more impact than viewing a film, though it wasn't always a pleasant one. It gave Emily the shudders seeing a flock of vultures waiting to feed on a fresh kill—horrible birds with their big bloated bodies and vicious looking beaks. On the other side of the spectrum were the giraffes—fascinating to watch a group of them amble along with a slow, stately grace, automatically evoking a smile.

On each of their trips out—different vehicles, different drivers—Emily was seated in the body of the van where a large section of the roof was lifted so passengers could stand up and take photographs. Zageo sat beside the driver, chatting to him about his life and work, observing how the safari session was handled—radio communication between the vans giving information about sightings so the drivers could change course, if necessary, to get to the scene as fast as they could.

Emily came to realise he didn't just check on the top-level management of his hotels. Nothing escaped his attention. He even stopped to talk to the employees who swept the paths to the rooms and it was not done in an autocratic manner. He accorded each person the same respect, none higher than another, and was clearly regarded with respect in return.

There was no shrugging or grimacing or rolling of eyes behind his back. He was liked, all the way down the line, and Emily couldn't help liking him, too, for the way he dealt with *his* people. It forced a revision of opinion on how he'd dealt with her.

In all honesty, she had to concede her story had probably sounded unbelievable. Zageo could well have been justified in not even listening to her, just handing her over to the police as an associate of Jacques Arnault. Instead of which, he'd given her the benefit of the doubt, proceeding to check the facts she'd given him while extending his highly generous and luxurious hospitality. Looked at objectively, this was more than fair treatment.

Except somehow none of it had been objective.

From the first moment of meeting it had been personal. Very, very personal. And it hadn't been all on his side, either. She'd been reacting against an attraction, an unwelcome one in both its strength and unsuitability, although when it came to a point of physical connection, she hadn't stopped him from kissing her. Now it was totally impossible to deny how much she wanted him to keep wanting her.

It even frightened her when he asked if she'd prefer to relax by the resort swimming pool, not accompany him on yet another safari trip. 'I thought you wanted me with you,' she answered anxiously, wondering if she had displeased him in some way.

He frowned, looking both exasperated and frustrated. 'You do not have to be a slave to me for your sister's sake,' he said tersely. 'I am here to carry out my responsibilities. I do not wish you to be bored, to put on a face of interest when you would rather be…'

'Bored?' Emily cried in astonishment. 'I'm not the least bit bored, Zageo.'

His dark intense eyes lasered hers for the truth. 'You have had day after day of rough travel. Perhaps you would like a long session of relaxing massages…'

'And miss out on seeing what I may never have the chance to see again? No way!' she asserted emphatically. 'I'm with you!'

A smile twitched at his lips. 'So. The adventure appeals.'

'I've always loved the world of nature. There's nothing in the animal kingdom I find boring,' Emily assured him.

One eyebrow arched. 'Including me?'

Him least of all, she thought, but looked askance at him, unwilling to give away too much. 'For me, *you* are an adventure, too, as I'm sure you're perfectly aware.'

Yes, he was, Zageo silently conceded.

And so was she for him—totally unlike any other woman he'd been with. Her lack of sexual sophistication had challenged him into making each new experience in the bedroom not only a titillating surprise for her but a sensual delight to be savoured over and over again. Her response was always intensely gratifying, sometimes quite intoxicating.

She also had a natural joy in life that revived his own. Gone was the jaded feeling with which he had left France to begin this trip. In fact, he was conscious of feeling a deeper pleasure in Emily Ross than any of the women who had preceded her. Which made it all the more vexing that she had come to him on such frustrating terms, denying him the satisfaction of winning her to his side.

She was happy enough to be there.

No doubt about that.

She didn't have enough artifice in her to pretend.

But would she have ever submitted to his will, given

there had been no problem with her sister, pushing a choice that might resolve it?

He hated this trade—hated it with a vengeance. He wanted done with it as fast as possible.

But Africa was Africa and very little moved at a fast pace. The days wore on with no progress towards an agreeable settlement between Malcolm Coleman and the hostile elements responsible for holding his family under house arrest.

Abdul was working overtime on pressing acceptable negotiations. The stumbling block was Coleman himself, not trusting anything he was offered and refusing to give up ownership of his farm. Abdul finally advised that direct confrontation would probably be required to gain an effective outcome.

'So a way to Coleman's farm must be cleared,' Zageo decided. 'Best to go in by helicopter.'

'But how not to get shot down?' Abdul muttered worriedly. 'I don't like this, Your Excellency. Why not explain to Miss Ross that her brother-in-law will not co-operate with the rescue plan? Perhaps she…'

'No!' Zageo flicked him a scornful look. 'Failure is unacceptable. The conference scheduled at our hotel in Zambia…find out what officials are coming from Zimbabwe and ensure that one of them has the power to grant me access with immunity. If you can also get some idea of what inducement would be welcome…'

Abdul nodded, looking relieved to be directed back into familiar territory.

Zageo reflected that this mission could end up costing him far more than he had anticipated. Endangering his own life was certainly going too far just to please a woman, yet there was no question in his mind that if it had to be done for Emily Ross, it had to be done. There had been no quarter asked in her giving to him, no excusing herself from anything he'd demanded of her, no protest at his leading her where she had not gone before. It was as though he had bought a slave. Which went against his every grain.

He *needed* this business finished.

Only after the trade had been honoured by him would he know if Emily Ross desired to stay at his side for reasons other than her sister's safety.

Emily couldn't help fretting over not knowing how things were for Hannah. She wished she could ask Zageo but he interpreted her need for information as a lack of trust in him. Having been sternly rebuffed for showing an impatience about getting results from his side of the bargain, she was wary of bringing up the subject again. However, his announcement that they would be flying on to Zambia instantly loosened her tongue.

They were in bed, relaxed after another exhilarating peak of intimacy, and Emily's mind leapt to a very different connection. 'Zambia and Zimbabwe share a border. Does this mean—?'

'It means we are going to Zambia,' he stated tersely, cutting off the spill of words from her.

Emily gritted her teeth as a wave of rebellion surged through her. She had been obedient to his wishes. She had been patient over the time he needed to clinch his side of the deal. But she was not going to be fobbed off as though she had no right to know what was happening with Hannah.

She heaved herself up, planting her hands on either side of his head, positioning herself directly above him for a very determined face-to-face encounter. 'What for?' she demanded.

His eyes glinted a deliberate challenge as he answered, 'One of our hotels is sited on the Zambezi River, just above Victoria Falls. It is on my itinerary.' ·

'So this move has nothing to do with my sister?'

'I will be meeting with people who may help.'

'May? *May?*' Her uncertainties coalesced into a shaft of anger. '*May* I remind you, Zageo, that you've had a very comprehensive downpayment on my side of our agreed trade and I have yet to receive any solid indication that you are doing anything productive on your side.'

'A downpayment!' he scoffed. 'Is that what you call doing what you want to do? Where's the cost to you, Emily? What have you paid?'

The counterattack was so swift and deadly, it threw her mind into chaos. Had it cost her anything to be with him? Not really. Which meant the trade wasn't equitable. And that left her without a reasonable argument. Panic whirled, wildly prompting action that might set the balance right again. She flung herself away from him, rolling off the bed, landing on her feet and backing away out of easy reach.

'So you think I would have said yes to you anyway.

Is that it, Zageo?' she fired at him. 'You think I find you irresistible?'

He propped himself up on his side, observing her with narrowed eyes. 'If there had been any resistance on your part, Emily, I would have been aware of it,' he mocked.

'Well, how about resistance now?'

'Don't be absurd.'

Emily steeled her backbone. Her eyes defied his arrogant confidence. He might be the most beautiful, sexiest man on earth but… 'I can say no to you,' she declared with enough ferocity to warn him she was serious.

His heavy-lidded gaze raked her naked body, reminding her of how intimately he knew it and how deeply he had pleasured it, sending her temperature sky-high in a rush of self-conscious guilt over her ready compliance to whatever pleased him.

'Why would you want to frustrate both of us?' he asked, his mouth curving into a sardonic little smile that derided such obvious foolishness.

Emily struggled to rise above the sexual pull of the man. If she didn't fight him now she would lose any bargaining power she had.

'You withhold information from me,' she swiftly accused. 'Why shouldn't I withhold myself from you until you share what I need to know?'

'So…we are back to bartering, are we?' Anger tightened his face and flashed from his eyes. 'There has been no progression in our relationship?'

'A relationship can only grow from sharing,' she hotly argued.

'Have I not shared much with you?'

'Yes,' she had to concede. 'But I want you to share what you're doing about Hannah and her family.'

Steely pride looked back at her. 'I have said I shall move them from harm's way and I will. That is all you need to know.'

'*Will!* And just how far in the future is that, Zageo?' She was on a roll now and nothing was going to stop her from pinning him down. Her pride was at stake, too. She had given herself to him in good faith and she was not going to be taken for a ride. '*Will* some action be taken from your hotel in Zambia?'

'Enough!'

He swung himself off the bed, rising to his feet with an autocratic hauteur that squeezed her heart and sent flutters through her stomach. His eyes blazed shrivelling scorn at her as he donned a robe, tying the belt with a snappy action—signal enough that the intimacy they had shared earlier was at a decisive end. He waved a dismissive hand over the bed.

'Consider it yours. I will not require any more *payment* from you…'

His tone was so savage it took Emily's breath away.

'…until you have received satisfaction from me,' he concluded bitingly, as though she had dismissed all the sexual satisfaction he'd given her as nothing worth having.

Emily sucked in some air, needing a blast of oxygen

to clear the shocked fog in her brain. 'I just want some news of Hannah!' she cried. 'Is that so unreasonable? Too much to ask when I'm so frightened for my sister?'

He ignored her, striding for the door which he clearly intended to put between them.

'I don't know where you're coming from, Zageo,' she hurled at his back. 'But where I come from we have a saying that every Australian understands and respects. *Fair go!* It's an intrinsic part of our culture—what we live by. And to me it's not fair of you to brush off my concern when I have tried my utmost to please you in every respect.'

He halted, his shoulders squaring with bunched tension. They rose and fell as he drew in and exhaled a very deep breath. His head did not turn. She could feel violence emanating from him as though it was a tangible thing, attacking her nerves and making them leap in a wild frenzy.

'No harm comes to the source of a lucrative deal while the deal is still pending,' he stated coldly. 'At this point in time, you need have no fear for your sister's life. Nor the lives of her husband and children.' He cast one hard glance at her as he added, 'We fly to Zambia in the morning. Be ready.'

Then he was gone.

CHAPTER FOURTEEN

I WILL be meeting with people who may help.

This must be it, Emily kept thinking, observing the preparations for a special dinner being set up on the perfectly manicured and very green lawn, which ran smoothly from the long line of white buildings comprising the hotel, right to the edge of the water. It was a fantastic site, overlooking the vast spread of the Zambezi River just before it plunged down a massive chasm, the spume from Victoria Falls sending up clouds of mist.

Government dignitaries from various African nations had been arriving all afternoon and the paths around the numerous units of accommodation were being patrolled by their security guards. A stage had been constructed under one of the large shade trees, facing the carefully arranged tables and chairs. Three African tenors were checking out the sound system, rehearsing some of the same operatic arias Emily had heard sung by the famous three—Pavarotti, Domingo and Carrera.

She had barely seen Zageo since they had arrived at this unbelievably beautiful place. He had appointed a hotel staff member to see to her every need and arrange whatever Emily wished to do. It felt as though he was divorcing himself from her.

Accommodation was designed in four suite units, two up, two down, each with a balcony or verandah with a direct view of the river. Emily was installed in an up-stairs suite and she knew Zageo was in the adjoining one but he had made no attempt to visit her.

Everything inside the suite was designed for two people; a king-size bed, two large lounging chairs with matching footstools, a very long vanity bench with two wash bowls in the spacious bathroom, plus a huge shower recess with a shower-head as large as a bread plate spraying out so much volume it gave one the sense of standing under a waterfall. So much luxury for one person felt very lonely.

Maybe after tonight—if he had a fruitful meeting— Zageo might deign to give her some news of what he was doing about Hannah's family. Emily could only hope so. Confronting him again would not elicit anything but another rebuff.

All along she had known there was a chasm of cultural differences between them, yet she had wanted him to deal with her as though he understood and shared her *Australian* attitudes. Big mistake! His way was *his* way and she had no choice but to accept that, especially with helping Hannah because she had no one else to turn to.

It was almost sunset. Drinks and canapés were being served from the bar at the back of the large wooden deck built around a large shade tree and extending over the edge of the river. Emily sat on a cushioned lounger, sipping a tropical fruit drink, listening to other guests commenting on the fantastic scenery.

The sky was streaked with vivid colour. About twenty metres away in the water was a raft of hippos, most of them submerged enough to look like a clump of rounded rocks. Much further away and silhouetted by the setting sun, a string of elephants started crossing the river from one island to another. Emily counted seven of them.

The splendour of Africa…

She fiercely wished Zageo was beside her, sharing it as they'd done in Kenya. She missed his company, his knowledge and experience, the excitement of his presence, the fine sexual tension that was constantly between them, promising more intimate pleasure to come as soon as they were alone together.

After two years of being single, with no inclination to join up with anyone, Emily realised that Zageo had well and truly revived her memory of what it was like to be in a relationship with a man—the physical, mental and emotional links that somehow made life more exhilarating. Even though common sense insisted this relationship could only be a temporary one, Emily had to acknowledge she didn't want it to end here.

It didn't matter how *foreign* Zageo was, in so many respects he was a marvellous person who lived an extraordinary life. She felt privileged to share just some of it with him. If he cast her off once he'd achieved his side of the trade…a sense of wretchedness clutched her heart.

She deeply regretted having reduced the sex they'd had to a form of prostitution, holding out for payment. The frustration of having no news of her sister's situation had driven her stance, not a lack of trust in Zageo's integrity. However, he'd clearly felt a strong sense of insult on two counts—her rejection of a natural outcome for their mutual attraction and her apparent disbelief in the keeping of his word.

Mistakes… Emily brooded over them, making herself more and more miserable as the evening wore on. She ordered a light dinner from room service but had no appetite for it. In her anguish over what was happening at the special outdoors dinner Zageo was attending, she switched off the lights in her suite and sat on the darkened balcony, watching the VIP guests below and trying to gauge if the meetings taking place were convivial or strained.

The three African tenors took turns in entertaining their audience, only coming together for a grand finale after coffee had been served. They were enthusiastically applauded, deservedly so, each one of them in marvellous voice. Once their concert was over, Emily trailed off to bed, having learnt nothing except for the firsthand observation that powerful people were royally entertained and probably expected it as their due.

Bed was the loneliest place of all. Her body yearned

to be once more intimately entangled with Zageo's, to feel all the intense and blissful sensual pleasure he had introduced her to. She tossed and turned for what seemed like hours. She didn't know when sleep finally overtook her restlessness, didn't know how long she had slept, didn't know what woke her.

There was no slow arousal from slumber, nothing pricking at her consciousness. It was as though a charge of electricity had thrown a switch to activate her. Her eyes snapped open. Her mind leapt to full alert.

The figure of a man was standing by the bed. The room was too dark to see his face but her heart did not flutter with fear. She knew instantly who it was. A surge of relief, hope and pleasure lilted through her voice.

'Zageo…' She pushed up from the pillow, propping herself on her elbows. 'I'm so glad you're here.'

Her gladness ran smack into a wall of tension, which seemed to suck it in and become even stronger, keeping him resolutely separate from her. It sparked a swift awareness that he had not meant to wake her, that he had come in the dead of night to look at her for some private reason and did not like being caught doing it.

Did he miss her, too?

Did he still want her as much as she wanted him?

Was pride forbidding him to admit it?

'Glad?' he fired back at her. 'Because you want news of your sister?'

His voice was clipped, angry, *hating* how his involvement with her now turned on the welfare of people he didn't even know.

Emily sat up, *hating* having dealt with him as she had. 'No,' she answered quietly, seriously. 'I'm sorry for…for making it sound as though being with you was only for the help you might give.'

There was a taut silence as he considered her apology. 'So…you admit this is not true?' His tone was more haughty this time, delivering scorn for the lie.

She heaved a rueful sigh. 'You know it's not true, Zageo.'

'Do not think I am deceived by this meek and mild act, Emily. If you imagine it might gain you more to butter me up than to demand…'

'No!' she cried in horror at his interpretation of her apology. 'I have really enjoyed your company and…and you're a fabulous lover, Zageo. I'll remember this time with you for the rest of my life, the pleasure you gave me…'

'Are you saying you no longer wish to withhold yourself from me?'

Emily took a deep breath, anxious to right the wrongs she'd done him and not caring how brazen she was about it. 'Yes,' she declared emphatically. 'I'd like you to come to bed with me right now.'

There! She couldn't be more positive than that! Her heart galloped as she waited for some response from him, frightened by his chilling stillness and frantically hoping for the desire he'd shown her to return in full force.

After an interminable few moments he spoke. 'You want me.'

Emily wasn't sure if it was a question or an ironic comment, but she answered without hesitation, 'Yes, I do.'

'Then show me how much, Emily.' No doubt about his tone now. It was hard and ruthless, challenging her mind, heart and soul. 'Show me that what I do tomorrow will not be done for nothing.'

Tomorrow…Hannah…the link burst through her brain, and on its heels came the red alert warning *not to ask*! If she brought her sister into this moment which was charged with explosive elements relating to only Zageo and herself, it would blow apart everything that could be good between them. Every instinct she had urged her to seize this night and make it theirs.

She swung her legs off the bed. He made no move towards her. His silence screamed of waiting…waiting to see how far *she* would go for *him*. Her eyes had become accustomed to the darkness, allowing her to see he was wearing the light cotton robe supplied by the hotel. No need for him to dress properly when the doors to their suites faced each other across the upstairs porch. Emily had no doubt he was naked underneath the robe.

She'd worn nothing to bed herself, hoping he might come. Any inhibitions about her body were long gone with Zageo. She was only too eager for him to touch it, caress it, pleasure it. But he didn't reach for her as she stepped close. He maintained an aloof stillness. Waiting…

Emily thought of how much he had *shown* her. Without the slightest hesitation she started undoing his tie belt. 'Were you lying in bed, thinking of what you could be doing with me?' she asked huskily, determined to seduce him out of this stand-off.

No reply.

'I was, for hours and hours,' she confessed, drawing his robe apart, sliding her hands up his chest, lightly rubbing her palms over his nipples. 'I wanted to feel you as I'm feeling you now.'

His chest lifted as his nipples hardened under her touch. The swift intake of breath was inaudible but his body revealed the signs of excitement. Emily moved around behind him and slid the robe down his arms, getting rid of the garment. Her hands went to work on the taut muscles of his neck and shoulders—a soft, sensual massage.

'Relax, Zageo,' she murmured. 'I don't want to fight you. I want to make love to you.'

He didn't relax. If anything, his muscles tightened even more.

She ran featherlight fingers down his back in soft whirling patterns, revelling in the satin smoothness of his skin as she gradually worked her way to his waist. Then she moved in, pressing her breasts against his sensitised back, gliding her hands around to the erotic zones on either side of his groin, caressing them, silently rejoicing in the tremors she raised with her touch.

'You've brought me back to life again,' she confided, trailing kisses down the curve of his spine. 'I've just been going through the motions for the past two years. Meeting you, knowing you…it came as a shock. I didn't know how to handle it, Zageo. But I do want you.' She pressed her cheek into the hollow between his shoulder blades, fervently murmuring, 'I do.'

His diaphram lifted with the quick refilling of his lungs with air. Emily moved her fingers lower, reaching for him, hoping she had aroused the desire he'd always *shown* her. Elation zinged through her as she felt his strong erection, the soft velvety skin stretched to contain the surge of his excitement.

Just the most delicate touch on the tip…and Zageo exploded into action, whirling around, seizing her waist, lifting her, carrying her headlong onto the bed with him, pinning her down, his eyes stabbing into hers with fierce intensity.

'Do not play with me, Emily. This has gone beyond games,' he stated harshly. 'Beyond anything civilised.'

'I wasn't playing with you,' she cried breathlessly.

'Then give me the new sense of life I gave you. I need it now. Now…'

He kissed her with a devouring passion that fired a tumultuous response from her. She wasn't trying to prove anything. Her own wild surge of need met his, fiercely demanding expression, craving satisfaction. His arms burrowed under her. She eagerly arched her body, wanting fierce collision, a swift primitive mating, the ecstatic sense of him driving into her.

It came and her body seemed to sing with exultation in his possession of her, her possession of him. It was marvellous, beautiful, glorious. She was hungry for the wonderfully intense feelings it generated, greedy for them. Her arms grasped him tightly. Her legs wound around him, urging him on, goading him on.

Zageo filled her with his power, lifted her onto wings of ecstasy that had her flying high, then swooping into delightful dips before soaring again, higher and higher until she simply floated in a delirium of pleasure, waiting for the ultimate fusion of his climax, the final fulfillment of their becoming one again.

When it came, to Emily it was sweeter than ever before. She hoped he felt as deeply moved by this special intimacy as she did. His forehead pressed briefly against hers, mind to mind, she thought, body to body. Then he heaved his weight off her, rolling, scooping her along with him, pressing her head over his heart, his fingers thrust into her hair, not stroking as he usually did, but grasping her scalp, holding her possessively against the thud of his life-beat.

He didn't speak.

Neither did she.

Emily was happy to have her head nestled precisely where it was. Her own heart kept time with his, giving her a blissful sense of harmony, the soft drumming gradually soothing her into a deep and peaceful sleep, cocooned securely in his embrace.

When he removed that embrace and left her, she had no idea. It was morning when she woke again and where he had lain in the bed was cold. For a few minutes she fretted over why he would have returned to his own suite instead of staying with her. Perhaps she hadn't answered his need. Perhaps…

Then she remembered.

Hannah!

Zageo had some action planned for tomorrow and now it was tomorrow. Last night she'd been certain it related to the trade they'd made. If that assumption was right, did he feel it was worth doing this morning? Was that why he was missing from her bed? He'd already gone about the business he had prearranged?

Emily rushed to the bathroom, anxious to be showered, dressed and ready for anything.

Today was important.

On how many counts she couldn't begin to guess.

CHAPTER FIFTEEN

EMILY braved knocking on the door to Zageo's suite, arguing to herself that last night's intimacy gave her the right to at least say hello. There was no response—disappointing, but to be expected, since it was almost nine o'clock and he was probably already attending to whatever he had planned for today.

A tense anticipation was jiggling her heart as she took the path to the central complex of the hotel. She wanted news of Hannah's situation but was frightened of what it might be. Something pertinent had transpired at last night's dinner or Zageo would not have come to her. From his attitude—from what he'd said—Emily sensed the news was not good. *The trade* was giving him more trouble than he'd bargained for.

Guests were breakfasting on the terrace and in the main restaurant. Neither Zageo nor his aide-de-camp, Abdul Haji, was amongst them. Emily walked on to the grand reception area—built like a pavilion with its splendid columns and open-air sides. She found Leila, the employee Zageo had appointed to look after her needs.

'Have you seen the sheikh this morning, Leila?'

'Yes. He left the hotel very early with Mr Haji.'

'How early?'

'At sunrise.'

'And they haven't returned,' Emily muttered, wondering if Zageo had left a message for her at reception.

'Mr Haji has,' came the helpful reply. 'I saw him walking by the river a little while ago. Would you like me to find him for you, Miss Ross?'

'No. No, thank you,' Emily answered quickly, acutely aware that Zageo's right hand man was not at her beck and call and would be affronted by such a move on her part. However, if she ran into him accidentally...

'Is there anything else I can do for you?' Leila inquired.

Emily flashed her a smile and shook her head. 'I think I'll just idle away this morning. Thanks again, Leila.'

Where would Zageo have gone by himself? The question teased her mind as she left the reception area, passing by the Livingstone Lounge—honouring the explorer, David Livingstone, who'd discovered and named Victoria Falls after the then Queen of England. It was furnished like a British colonial club room with many groups of leather chairs and sofas, card tables, chess tables, mahjong tables, plus a bar at the end—all designed to cater for every recreational taste. A glance at the few occupants assured her the black bearded Abdul Haji was not present.

She stood on the terrace, looking from left to right, hoping to spot the man. To the left, the view along the river was unobscured. Everything from last night's dinner and entertainment had been cleared away, leaving nothing but pristine green lawn and the magnificent shade trees. She saw no one taking a stroll in that direction.

To the right there were more trees, plus the cabana providing service to the swimming pool, and closer to the river bank two white marquees where various types of massages were on offer. If Abdul Haji was still walking, Emily decided it had to be somewhere beyond the marquees.

Five minutes later, Emily spotted him, leaning on the railing of a small jetty, apparently watching the swirl of the water as it rushed towards the fall. He caught sight of her approach and straightened up, focusing his attention on her with what felt like a hostile intensity, which was highly disquieting. She hesitated on the bank beside the jetty, torn between her need to know about Zageo and the sense of being distinctly unwelcome.

Abdul Haji frowned, made an impatient gesture and tersely said, 'There is no news. We must wait.'

It seemed that Abdul thought she knew more than she did. Hoping to elicit some information, she prompted, 'Zageo left at sunrise.'

Hands were thrown up in disgust. 'It is madness, this adventure—' his eyes flashed black resentment at her '—flying directly to the farm over the heads of Zimbabwe officialdom. What if your brother-in-law persists in not seeing reason, even when your passport is shown to him? So much risk for nothing.'

Shock rolled through Emily's mind and gripped her heart. Zageo was putting his own life at hazard to keep his word to her. It was too much. She would never have asked it of him. Never!

Diplomatic connections…bribery…deals under tables…big money talking as it always did…all these things she had imagined happening, but no real personal risk. However, the comment about Malcolm not seeing reason suggested that Hannah's husband hadn't cooperated with what had been initiated to help the family's situation. And Emily realised her own attitude about *payment* had virtually forced Zageo to deliver.

'I'm sorry,' she blurted out, her own anxiety for his safety rising. 'I didn't mean for it to go this far.'

Abdul glared a dismissal of her influence. 'His Excellency, the sheikh, does as he wishes.'

'Yes, of course,' she agreed, not about to argue against male supremacy in this instance. 'It's just that if we hadn't met…'

'It is futile to rail against Fate.'

Emily took a deep breath as she tried to stop floundering and gather her wits. 'I didn't realise Malcolm would cause problems.'

'A man does not easily give up what is his. This I understand. But Malcolm Coleman must be made to understand that the loss is inevitable. There is no choice,' Abdul said fiercely. 'That was made very clear last night.'

The meeting…Zageo coming to her afterward…deciding what had to be done to honour his side of their trade.

Emily felt sick. 'I shouldn't have asked him to help.'

Abdul frowned at her. 'You made a request?'

'Yes,' she confessed miserably. 'After I'd received the e-mail from my sister…when we met for dinner that evening—'

'The decision was already made,' Abdul cut in, waving a dismissal of her part in promoting this action.

Flutters attacked her stomach. 'What do you mean…*already made*?'

'On his return to the palace from your visit to The Salamander Inn, His Excellency sought me out and ordered a preliminary investigation into ways to secure the safety of your sister and her family,' Abdul curtly informed her.

'Before dinner?' Emily queried incredulously.

'It was late afternoon. His Excellency wished to alleviate your distress, Miss Ross. Surely he told you so when you met that evening.'

She'd rushed straight into the trade!

It hadn't even occurred to her that Zageo might care enough—on such short acquaintance—to initiate action which might give her some peace of mind about her sister. No wonder he'd been angry at her assumption that he'd only do it to have sex with her.

'Yes, he did say he'd help,' she muttered weakly.

'These are difficult times in Zimbabwe. Our negotiations kept breaking down. It has been very frustrating,' Abdul muttered in return.

And on their last night in Kenya she had more or less accused Zageo of doing nothing!

She'd been so wrong. So terribly, terribly wrong.

Feeling totally shattered by these revelations, Emily almost staggered over to a nearby bench seat and sank onto it, her legs having become too rubbery to keep standing.

'He took my passport to identify himself as a friend to Hannah and Malcolm?' she asked.

'It is to be hoped it will satisfy.' Abdul frowned at her again. 'You did not know this?'

'Zageo said he had something planned for today but he gave no precise details.'

'All going well, he intends to fly them out.'

'Without…' She swallowed hard. 'Without permission from the authorities?'

'A blind eye may be turned but I have no reason to trust these people.' The signature tune of a mobile telephone alerted him to a call. 'Please excuse me, Miss Ross,' he said, whipping the small communicator out of his shirt pocket and striding to the end of the jetty to ensure a private conversation.

Emily waited in tense silence, hoping—fearing— this was news of Zageo's rescue mission being transmitted. Abdul had his back turned to her so she could neither hear him speak or see his expression. Her heart jumped as he wheeled around, tucking the telephone back in his pocket.

'We go,' he called, waving her to join him as he strode back to the river bank, clearly galvanised into action.

Adrenaline surged through Emily as she leapt to her feet. 'Go where?'

'To the landing pad. Your presence is required there.'

'Landing pad?'

'For the helicopter,' he explained impatiently, probably thinking her dim-witted.

Emily had imagined Zageo was using his private aeroplane, but a helicopter definitely made more sense in the circumstances—a much quicker in and out. *If* Malcolm and Hannah had co-operated in leaving the farm with Zageo.

She half-ran to keep up with Abdul as he headed up to the hotel. 'So Zageo is on his way back?' she asked breathlessly.

'Yes. But not yet out of danger. He is using one of the helicopters that normally flies tourists around and over Victoria Falls. It allows some leeway over Zimbabwe airspace but not as much as this flight has taken.'

Could it be shot down?

Emily couldn't bring herself to raise that question, though she felt compelled to ask, 'Is my sister…?'

'They are all in the helicopter,' came the curt reply. 'It will be reassuring for the Coleman family to see you, Miss Ross.'

'Right!' she muttered, thinking what black irony it was that *they* didn't completely trust Zageo's word, either.

Guilt and shame wormed through her. She had not credited Zageo with compassionate caring nor with the kind of integrity that went beyond any normal expectation. He was not only a man of great character, but the most generous person she had ever known. Given another chance, she would show him an appreciation that went far beyond the bedroom.

At the hotel entrance a driver and minibus were waiting to transport them to the helicopter base. This was only a fifteen-minute trip from the hotel and neither Abdul nor Emily spoke on the way. Once there, they were met by the base manager and escorted straight through the waiting lounge where groups of tourists were gathered for their sightseeing flights.

As soon as they were outside again and taking the path to the landing pad, their escort pointed to a black dot in the sky. 'That's it coming in now.'

'No problems?' Abdul asked.

The base manager shrugged. 'Not in the air. Our best pilot is at the controls.'

The limited answer worried Emily. 'Are any of the passengers injured?'

'Not to my knowledge. There was no call for medical aid,' came the reassuring reply.

They waited near the end of the path, watching the black dot grow larger and larger. Emily felt a churning mixture of excitement and apprehension. While she desperately wanted to see Hannah and her family safe and sound, would they thank her for interfering in their lives? Zageo had acted on her behalf, probably being very forceful, intent on *showing* her he did deliver on his word. She could only hope this dramatic rescue had been the right action to take.

The wind from the whirling helicopter blades plastered her clothes against her body and blew her hair into wild disarray but Emily maintained her stance, facing the landing so she was immediately recognisable to her sister. She could now see Hannah in the cabin, directly behind Zageo who was seated beside the pilot.

At last the helicopter settled on the ground. The base manager moved forward to open the door and assist the passengers in disembarking. Zageo was out first. He gave Emily a searing look that burnt the message into her brain—*payment made in full*! Then he turned to help Hannah out, delivering the sister who had not made it to Zanzibar—the sister who had inadvertently brought Emily into his life.

But would he want her to stay in it?

CHAPTER SIXTEEN

EMILY had found it a strangely fraught day. While there had been joy in the reunion with her sister and relief that the rescue had been very timely according to Malcolm, who was immensely grateful to have his family brought to a safe place, she was wracked with uncertainty over where she stood with Zageo.

He had bowed out of any further involvement with her family once they had been brought to the hotel and given accommodation. 'I'm sure you'll want some private time together,' he'd said, making no appointment with Emily for some time alone with him.

Naturally the moment he had excused himself from their presence, Hannah had pounced with a million questions about *the sheikh* and Emily's involvement with such an unlikely person, given her usual circle of acquaintances.

Where had she met him?

How long had she known him?

What was their relationship?

Why would he do so much for her?

The worst one was—You didn't sell yourself to him, did you, Em?—spoken jokingly, though with a wondering look in her eyes.

She had shrugged it off, saying, 'Zageo is just very generous by nature.'

'And drop-dead gorgeous.' Hannah's eyes had rolled knowingly over what she rightfully assumed was a sexual connection. 'Quite a package you've got there. Are you planning on hanging onto him?'

'For as long as I can,' she'd answered, acutely aware that her time with Zageo might well have already ended.

A big grin bestowed approval. 'Good for you! Not, I imagine, a forever thing, but certainly an experience to chalk up—being with a real life sheikh!'

Not a forever thing… Her sister's comment kept jangling in her mind. Having said good-night to Hannah and Malcolm and their beautiful little daughters, Emily walked slowly along the path to her own accommodation, reflecting on how she had believed her marriage to Brian was to be forever. The words—*Till death do us part*—in the marriage service had meant fifty or sixty years down the track, not a fleeting few.

It was impossible to know what the future held. Life happened. Death happened. It seemed to her there were so many random factors involved, it was probably foolish to count on anything staying in place for long. With today's technology, the world had become smaller, its pace much faster, its boundaries less formidable. Even culture gaps were not as wide. Or maybe she just wanted to believe that because the thought of being separated from Zageo hurt.

She wanted more of him.

A lot more.

On every level.

Having arrived on the porch outside the doors to both Zageo's suite and hers, she decided to knock on his, hoping to have some direct communication with him about today's events. Disappointment dragged at her heart when there was no response.

She tried arguing to herself that he had come into her suite last night and would come again if he wanted to. There was no point in chasing after him. It hadn't worked for Veronique and Emily had no doubt it wouldn't work for her, either. When Zageo decided it was time up on a relationship, that was it.

Tomorrow his private jet was to fly Hannah and Malcolm and the girls to Johannesburg, from where they would catch a commercial flight to Australia. For all Emily knew, she might be expected to go with them. With the depressing thought that this could be her last night anywhere near Zageo, she turned to her own door, unlocked it and entered the suite which she knew was bound to feel even more lonely tonight…unless he came.

He didn't come.

He was already there.

As Emily stepped past the small foyer and into the bed-sitting room, Zageo entered it from the balcony where she had sat watching last night's special dinner. She wanted to run to him, fling her arms around his neck and plaster his face with wildly grateful kisses for his extraordinary kindnesses to her family. It would have been the natural thing to do if everything had been natural between them. But it wasn't. Because of the trade *she* had initiated. So she stood with her feet rooted to the floor, waiting to hear her fate from him.

He didn't move towards her, either, standing stiffly proud and tall just inside the room, his brilliant dark eyes watching her with an intensity that played havoc with every nerve in her body. If he still felt desire for her, it was comprehensively guarded.

'Is all well with your sister and her family?' he asked, his tone coolly polite.

'Thanks to you, Zageo, as well as it can be, given such a traumatic upheaval to their lives,' she answered quietly.

'In the end there was no choice but to accept the upheaval,' he stated unequivocally. 'Your brother-in-law was a marked man, Emily.'

'Yes. So I understand. And while I will be eternally grateful you did go in and get them out, when I made the…the deal…with you, I didn't expect you to endanger your own life, Zageo. I thought—' she gestured a sense of helplessness over his decision to act himself '—I thought something more impersonal would be worked.'

His eyes blazed a fierce challenge. 'Was it impersonal…your joining your body to mine?'

'No! I…'

'Then why would you expect me to do less than you?'

'I didn't mean…' She stopped, took a deep breath, and desperately not wanting to argue with him, simply said, 'I was frightened for you.'

His head tilted to one side consideringly. 'You cared for my safety?'

'Of course I did!'

'As, no doubt you would for anyone in danger,' he concluded dismissively.

It wiped out what she'd been trying to get across to him. How could she build bridges if Zageo was intent on smashing them? Before she could come up with some winning approach he spoke with a chilling finality.

'Nevertheless, all is well that ends well. You no longer have anything to fear, Emily.'

Except losing him from her life.

He gestured towards the writing desk. 'There is your passport. Now that our trade is complete, you are free to go wherever you like. Perhaps to Johannesburg with your sister tomorrow.'

Her inner anguish spilled out, needing to hear the truth from him. 'You don't want me with you anymore?'

A blaze of anger answered her. 'Do not turn this onto me. You have said over and over again I give you no choice.' He flung out an arm as though releasing her from all bondage to him. 'Go where you will. I free you of any sense of obligation to me.'

She lifted her own arms in an impassioned plea. 'I want to go with you, Zageo. Wherever you go.'

He gave her a savage look. 'For as long as it suits

you, Emily? To see more of Africa and do it in the style I can provide?'

'I wouldn't care if we were doing it on a shoestring budget. I want more of you, Zageo,' she cried recklessly.

'Ah! So it is the sex you want more of,' he mocked. 'The pleasures of the flesh are enticing, are they not?'

'Yes,' she flung back at him, seizing on his mocking statement to fight his stand-off position. 'That was what enticed you into keeping hold of me in the first place, and it didn't seem to me you were tired of what I could provide for you last night.'

His eyes narrowed. 'Most men facing possible death would want to have sex beforehand.'

She burned, hating the humiliating minimalisation of what they'd shared. 'You were just using me? Is that what you're saying, Zageo?'

'You do not care to be used, Emily?'

The message was scorchingly clear.

He'd hated being used by her.

The heat in her cheeks was painful, but she would not drop her gaze from his, determined on resolving the issues between them. 'I'm sorry. Mr Haji told me this morning you had intended to help with Hannah's situation anyway. Believe me, I already feel wretched over misjudging the kind of person you are. My only excuse is…I thought the way you dealt with Veronique meant dealing with me in the same way would not be unusual for you.'

He gave a derisive snort. 'I knew what I was buying into with Veronique. You, my dear Emily, did not fit any mould I was familiar with.'

'Well, if I surprised you, multiply that surprise by about a million and you might approach how big a surprise you've been to me,' she retorted with feeling. 'Talk about being in foreign territory with a foreigner…'

'Yes!' His eyes fiercely raked her up and down. 'Extremely foreign territory with a foreigner!'

'But we have found a lot of mutual ground, haven't we?' she quickly appealed. 'And we might find even more pleasure in everything if we stay together. And I don't mean only in bed, so if you think I want to tag along with you just for the sex…'

She ran out of breath. The tension in the room seemed to have a stranglehold on any free flow of oxygen. In fact, Emily felt hopelessly choked up and couldn't think what else to say anyway.

'Do I understand you now wish to accompany me on this journey without fear or favour?' Zageo asked, cocking an eyebrow as though merely ascertaining her position, certainly not giving away his own.

Emily swallowed hard and managed to produce a reply. 'I'd like to try it.'

'Being companions and lovers.'

'Yes.'

'No more bartering.'

'No. Complete freedom of choice.'

Let this woman go, Zageo fiercely berated himself. *No more talk. No more delay. Let her go now*!

'Emily, freedom of choice is a myth. There is no such thing, not in your culture nor mine. We are bound into attitudes and values by our upbringing and we think and act accordingly.'

Her beautiful blue eyes begged a stay of judgment. 'But we can learn more about each other, try to understand where we're both coming from, be willing to make compromises…'

She was still tugging on him, getting under his skin. 'No,' he said emphatically. Abdul was right. His mind was barely his own around this woman. She drove him into excesses. He had to put a stop to it, regain control, make sensible decisions. 'What we came together for… it is done, Emily.'

Her shoulders slumped. There was a flash of anguish on her face before her head bowed in defeat. 'So this is goodbye,' she said in a desolate little voice.

'Yes,' he said firmly, hating seeing her like this. She was a fighter, strong, resilient, resourceful. She had challenged him to the limit and beyond. Whatever she was feeling right now, she would get over it and move on.

As he must.

Zageo propelled his feet forward, determined on walking out of this suite, walking out of her life. It was better that the power she had exerted over him was brought to a close. Though he couldn't help thinking there was a bitter irony in her surrendering to his will at the end. He didn't like it. He liked it even less when a glance at her in passing showed tears trickling through her lowered lashes and down her cheeks.

Silent tears.

She had dignity.

Dignity that pulled hard on him.

Emily Ross was not just sexually desirable. She was a very special woman, unique in his experience. When she gave of herself, she gave everything.

He reached the door.

There was no sound behind him. No movement.

Did he really want to give up what he'd found in Emily? Did such a decision make him master of his life or did it make him less of a man for not meeting the challenge of keeping her at his side?

He sucked in a deep breath, needing the blast of oxygen to clear the feverish thoughts attacking what had seemed so clear to him all day. His hand was on the doorknob, ready to turn it. A few more seconds and his exit would be effected. No going back.

'I forgot to say thank you,' she jerked out huskily. 'Not for my sister and her family. For me. All you did for me. Thank you, Zageo.'

The emotion in her voice curled around his heart, squeezing it unmercifully. His brain closed down, instinct taking over, driving his legs back to where she still stood with her head bent in hopeless resignation. He grabbed her waist, spun her around, clamped her to him with one arm, cupped her chin with his hand.

'Look at me!' he commanded.

She raised startled, tear-washed eyes.

'I have decided our journey should not end here. We shall continue to be companions and lovers if you find this arrangement agreeable.'

Sparkles of joyful relief shone back at him. Her arms flew up around his neck, hooking it tightly. The soft lushness of her breasts heaved against his chest, reminding him how very delectable they were, as was the rest of her.

'Sounds good to me,' she whispered seductively, no hesitation at all about surrendering to his will, which Zageo liked very much this time. Very much indeed.

It drew his mouth to hers, the desire to taste and savour her giving was totally overwhelming, obliterating any possible second thoughts about having changed his mind.

It was a kiss worth having.

Emily Ross was a woman worth having.

And have her he would, regardless of where it led.

At least until this passion had spent itself and he was free and in control of himself again.

CHAPTER SEVENTEEN

THE last hotel, Emily thought, looking out the tall windows of their suite, taking in the sparkling view of Cape Town's waterfront. Their journey through Africa had been amazing—so many different facets of the country from wonderful wildlife to highly cultivated wineries—but it was coming to an end now. Once Zageo was satisfied that all was well with this perfectly sited boutique hotel, the next stop would be Dubai.

Emily didn't know how their relationship was going to work in Zageo's home territory. Perhaps he would decide to house her in Paris or London, avoiding too big a cultural clash. Emily didn't mind what he arranged as long as they remained lovers. The thought of having no part of his life was unbearable.

'I see Veronique wasted little time in mourning my departure,' Zageo drawled sardonically.

The mention of his former mistress sent a frisson of shock down Emily's spine. She'd just been thinking of Paris and now she was reminded that the model had been with Zageo for two years. Would her own relationship with him last that long?

Behind her came the rustle of the English newspaper he'd been reading over his after breakfast coffee. 'According to this report, she's about to marry the German industrialist, Claus Eisenberg. It will be his third trophy wife but I don't imagine Veronique is looking for lasting love so they will probably suit each other well.'

His mocking tone goaded her into asking, 'Do you believe that love can last, Zageo?'

The impulsive question was driven by her deep sense of vulnerability about her future with him and she hoped for a serious reply, needing some guide to where they were heading together.

'Yes,' he asserted strongly. 'I do believe it can. My mother and father are still devoted to each other.'

While this statement did not relate to her in any way, it lifted Emily's heart and she turned around, smiling at him. 'That's really nice.'

He smiled back. 'We do have that in common since your own parents are content with their marriage. And speaking of them—' he waved towards the computer notepad he'd acquired for her use '—you haven't checked your mail this morning.'

'I'll do it now.'

She crossed to the writing desk where the small slimline computer was set up, ready for her to connect with the Internet. As she switched on and started keying in her password, she was very conscious that this was yet another example of Zageo's generosity and his caring consideration for her needs, ensuring she had electronic access to her family at any time of the day or night.

She hadn't asked for it. She hadn't asked Zageo for any of the things he'd bought for her along the way. He'd taken her shopping for clothes whenever he'd considered her own outfits unsuitable for *his* companion and Emily had argued to herself she was indulging his pleasure in her, not taking him for all she could get. The clothes were unreturnable but this computer could be passed to Abdul Haji if and when Zageo said her time with him was over.

She wasn't like Veronique.

She had come to love Zageo with all her heart.

'There's a message from Hannah,' she said, wanting to share everything with him.

'Any news?'

'Malcolm is happy to get into the sugar industry, managing Dad's cane farm. Jenny and Sally have started at a playschool to get them used to being with other children and they've both found best friends to play with. And Hannah…oh, how wonderful!' She clapped her hands in delight and swung around, beaming a big grin at Zageo. 'Hannah's pregnant!'

'That's good?' he quizzed with a bemused air.

'She wanted to try for a boy, but Malcolm was worried about her going through another pregnancy when the situation in Zimbabwe was so unstable. Besides, he insisted he was perfectly happy with his girls and didn't need a boy.'

'All children are precious,' Zageo commented.

'Yes, but having been just two sisters ourselves, Hannah and I always fancied having mixed families. I do hope it's a boy for her this time.'

'You wouldn't mind having three children yourself?'

'Actually I think four is the perfect number. Two of each.'

'Four has always been a very significant number,' Zageo mused. 'Did you know it resonates through all the religions of mankind?'

'No, I didn't.'

'Even in your Christian religion, it comes up over and over again—forty days and forty nights in the desert, the four horsemen of the apocalypse…'

Emily's interest was captivated as he went on, spelling out the commonality that underpinned so much of what the people of the world believed in. Zageo was far more broadly educated than herself and he often expounded on fascinating pieces of knowledge. She couldn't help thinking he would be a marvellous father and fiercely wished she could be the mother of his children.

He suddenly stopped theorising and smiled at her, bestowing a sense of warm approval that made Emily tingle with pleasure. 'There's a place I'd like to show you today. Let's get ready to go, once you've replied to Hannah. And please send my congratulations to her and Malcolm.'

'Will do.'

She turned back to the computer notepad, happy to write her own congratulations as well as his and eager to go wherever Zageo wanted to take her.

When they emerged from the hotel, a gorgeous yellow Mercedes convertible with blue and black leather upholstery was waiting for them. 'Wow!' Emily cried excitedly as the doorman led the way to it. 'Is this for us?'

Zageo laughed at her burst of pleasure. 'It's a beautiful day, we will be driving down the coast, and I thought we should have a happy sunshine car to make it a more exhilarating trip,' he said.

'What a great idea! I love it!' Emily enthused, having long given up protesting Zageo's extravagance over anything he did with her. Over the past three months of being with him, she'd learnt that what gave him pleasure invariably gave her pleasure so it made no sense to fight it.

It was, indeed, an exhilarating trip, all the way to Cape Point which offered a spectacular view over the Cape of Good Hope, the southernmost point of Africa. The peninsula ended in a high cliff, on top of which stood a lighthouse. It was clearly a popular tourist spot. Numerous flights of steps led up to it and there was a funicular to transport those who didn't want to do the long climb.

'Would you like to ride or walk?' Zageo asked.

'Walk,' Emily decided. 'We can take our time enjoying the view from all the rest stops along the way.'

He took her hand, encasing it firmly with his. Emily loved the physical link with him. Somehow it was more than just companionable. It felt as though he was laying claim to her in a much deeper sense. Or maybe she was reading into it what she wanted to.

Just savour this time with him, she told herself, and make the most of each day as it comes. Hadn't she learnt from losing Brian so young that it was important to live the moment, not spend it counting her tomorrows?

Yet even as she enthused over the spectacular vista of cliffs and ocean, she couldn't help commenting, 'You really should visit Australia, Zageo. It has the most brilliant coastline in the world. Just north of Cairns we have the Forty Mile Beach, all clean white sand. The Great Ocean Road down in Victoria with the fantastic rock formations called the Twelve Apostles rising out of the sea, is just breathtaking. Not to mention…'

She ran off at the mouth, encouraged by the warm pleasure that danced over her from his twinkling eyes. 'If you would be happy to show me, I would be happy to come,' he said when she'd finished her tourist spiel, making her heart swell with joy. It was clear proof that he saw no end for their relationship in the near future.

Emily's delight in the day increased a hundredfold. Having been assured that this last tip of the African continent had no personal relevance as far as she Zageo were concerned, she could barely stop her feet from galloping up the last flight of steps to the top viewing area around the lighthouse.

They moved to the furthermost point and she stood against the stone safety wall, cocooned from the other tourists by Zageo who stood closely behind her, his arms encircling her waist, making her feel they were on top of the world together.

'Here we are at the Cape of Good Hope and you are looking down at where two great oceans meet, Emily,' he murmured, his head lowered to rub his cheek against her hair, his soft breath making her ear tingle.

'There should be some sign of it,' she mused. 'Waves clashing or different water colours mingling.'

'Instead there is a harmonious flow, a union that does not break because of coming from different places. This is how nature ordains it. It is only people who make demarcations.'

Emily sighed at this truth. Why couldn't the stream of humanity recognise its natural commonality instead of dividing itself into hostile camps?

'Are you brave enough to merge your life with mine, Emily?'

Her heart leapt. Her mind frantically quizzed what he meant. Hadn't she already merged her life with his?

'I'm brave enough to do anything with you, Zageo,' she answered, her stomach fluttering nervously over whether this was what he wanted to hear. She had the frightening sense that something critical was coming.

His arms tightened around her, pulling her body back into full contact with his. He kissed the lobe of her ear and whispered, 'Regardless of the differences that have shaped our lives, we have that natural flow, Emily. So I ask…will you marry me and be the mother of my children? Stand with me, no matter what we face in the future? Stand together as we are now.'

The shock of hearing a proposal she had never expected completely robbed Emily of any breath to answer. Her body whipped around in his embrace, her arms lifting to fly around his neck, instinctively grabbing for every linkage to him. Her eyes drank in the blaze of love and desire in his, taking all the fierce courage and determination she needed from it.

'Yes, I can do that, Zageo,' she said with absolute assurance. 'I will do it,' she promised him. 'I love you with all that I am.'

Sheikh Zageo bin Sultan Al Farrahn looked into the shining blue eyes of the woman who had made it impossible for him to choose any other woman to share his life. He remembered arrogantly determining to put her in her place, not realising at the time that her place would be at his side. He had decided to find a *suitable* wife, and he had found in Emily Ross a true compatibility in everything he really valued.

He lifted a hand to stroke her cheek in a tender caress, wanting to impart how very precious she was to him. 'And I love you with all that I am,' he replied, cherishing her words to him, repeating them because they carried a truth which should be spoken and always acknowledged between them.

A lasting love…

A love that no force could touch because they willed it so…together.

UNcut

Even more passion for your reading pleasure!

You'll find the drama, the emotion, the international
settings and the happy endings that you love
in Harlequin Presents. But we've turned up the
thermostat a little, so that the relationships really
sizzle.... Careful, they're almost too hot to handle!

Are you ready?

"Captive in His Bed weaves together romance,
passion, action adventure and espionage into
one thrilling story that will keep you turning the
pages...Sandra Marton does not disappoint."
—Shannon Short, *Romantic Times BOOKclub*

CAPTIVE IN HIS BED
by Sandra Marton

on sale May 2006

*Look out for the next thrilling
Knight brothers story, coming in July!*

www.eHarlequin.com

HPUC0506

If you enjoyed what you just read,
then we've got an offer you can't resist!

Take 2 bestselling love stories FREE!

Plus get a FREE surprise gift!

Clip this page and mail it to Harlequin Reader Service®

IN U.S.A.	IN CANADA
3010 Walden Ave.	P.O. Box 609
P.O. Box 1867	Fort Erie, Ontario
Buffalo, N.Y. 14240-1867	L2A 5X3

YES! Please send me 2 free Harlequin Presents® novels and my free surprise gift. After receiving them, if I don't wish to receive anymore, I can return the shipping statement marked cancel. If I don't cancel, I will receive 6 brand-new novels every month, before they're available in stores! In the U.S.A., bill me at the bargain price of $3.80 plus 25¢ shipping & handling per book and applicable sales tax, if any*. In Canada, bill me at the bargain price of $4.47 plus 25¢ shipping & handling per book and applicable taxes**. That's the complete price and a savings of at least 10% off the cover prices—what a great deal! I understand that accepting the 2 free books and gift places me under no obligation ever to buy any books. I can always return a shipment and cancel at any time. Even if I never buy another book from Harlequin, the 2 free books and gift are mine to keep forever.

106 HDN DZ7Y
306 HDN DZ7Z

Name	(PLEASE PRINT)	
Address	Apt.#	
City	State/Prov.	Zip/Postal Code

Not valid to current Harlequin Presents® subscribers.

Want to try two free books from another series?
Call 1-800-873-8635 or visit www.morefreebooks.com.

* Terms and prices subject to change without notice. Sales tax applicable in N.Y.
** Canadian residents will be charged applicable provincial taxes and GST.
All orders subject to approval. Offer limited to one per household.
® are registered trademarks owned and used by the trademark owner and or its licensee.

PRES04R   ©2004 Harlequin Enterprises Limited

**The Scorsolini Princes:
proud rulers and passionate lovers
who need convenient wives!**

Welcome to this brand-new miniseries,
set in glamorous and exotic places—it's
a world filled with passion, romance and royals!

Don't miss this new trilogy by

Lucy Monroe

THE PRINCE'S VIRGIN WIFE
May 2006

HIS ROYAL LOVE-CHILD
June 2006

THE SCORSOLINI MARRIAGE BARGAIN
July 2006